MW00936142

GASPAR BROWN

ADVENTURE 4

More Gaspar Brown Adventures

by

Hutton Wilkinson

GASPAR BROWN

AND

THE HOUSE

OF MYSTERY

ADVENTURE 4

HUTTON WILKINSON

Gaspar Brown and the House of Mystery
© 2020 Hutton Wilkinson

This is a work of fiction. All of the characters, organizations, and events portrayed in this novel are either products of the author's imagination or are used fictitiously. Any resemblance to actual persons, living or dead, businesses, companies, events, or locales is entirely coincidental.

Book design by Sue Campbell Book Design

ISBN 13: 978-1-7325653-3-3 (print)

Contents

GASPAR'S STORY SO FAR

WHEN Gaspar Brown, boy billionaire, returned to Perdido Isle from his big Antarctic adventure, it marked the beginning of his second year, living on the Gulf of Mexico in Florida. Perdido Isle, the 500,000-acre domain that Gaspar had recently inherited was a magical place full of discovery for him and his pal Alex.

Since arriving on Perdido Isle, Gaspar solved *The Mystery of the Gasparilla Succession*, by thwarting Unzega, the evil Yucatan drug lord. Later, with the help of his friends, Gaspar assisted the local police in bringing down a ring of jewel thieves that had been the scourge of the Florida coast from Naples to Pensacola. The discovery and return of the hoard of looted sparklers in *The*

Mystery of the Seminole Spring, subsequently led Gaspar to Antarctica where, with Alex and his pal Brewster Wharton in tow, they went in search of Nazi gold, as well as a stolen copy of the legendary *Necronomicon*.

Before returning back to Florida, the adventurous teenagers had not only solved *The Mystery of the Necronomicon*, but had explored Buenos Aires and its environs as well as Antarctica. On top of all this excitement, Gaspar was still in the middle of restoring his great Uncle Charlie's Edwardian yacht *Floridablanca*, built in 1910. Eugenia Floride, Uncle Charlie's adopted daughter had re-Christened the yacht *Argent* and then deliberately sank her, after filling the hold with a fortune in museum quality silver objects shortly before her death. Gaspar knew that restoring the yacht would be no easy task, and had put the project in the capable hands of his friend, and sailing instructor, Captain Craig Cadawalader.

Perdido isle is joined to the mainland of Coral County, Florida by a causeway over an inland waterway. The causeway connects with a road cutting directly through the town of Calaluna, one of two towns on the 500-acre island. Both of the privately-owned island's towns had been built in the 1920s by Gaspar's eccentric great Uncle, Charles Muñoz Flores y Gaspar. Uncle Charlie built Calaluna as a working-class town in a Spanish revival style consisting of a grid of eight boulevards intersected by ten avenues.

Slicing through the middle of the town going east and west lay Center Street, and bisecting that thoroughfare going north and south was State Street, the main business street of Calaluna. Each of the towns consisted of 50,000 acres, which Uncle Charlie had leased to the happy citizens of Perdido Isle in the 1920s for 99 years at a rate of one dollar per acre per month.

Llojeta, the other town on the island is situated at the eastern end of Perdido Isle. A resort town, Llojeta inhabited seasonally by visitors, mostly from New York, seeking the rarified atmosphere provided by its fantasy Venetian inspired pink and white architecture. The grid pattern of this 50,000-acre town is laid out similarly to that of Calaluna, but the names of the streets are inspired by romantic Italian *Via's* rather than simple Spanish *Calle's*.

Since arriving on Perdido Isle, teenaged Gaspar Brown longs to explore each and every street and parcel of land, to better understand the scope of his inheritance, which includes La Rinconada, the amazing house and grounds where he lives with his mother, Elvira. Also at La Rinconada lives Gaspar's best friend and sidekick, Alex Mendoza and his parents, the property's caretakers, Felix and Angela.

La Rinconada is a vast estate that Gaspar feels he scarcely knows, let alone the nuances of the two towns. After school and on weekends, he and Alex had cover a lot of ground on their bicycles as well as in the old woody station wagon that the boys had fixed up with the help of Gaspar's driver and mechanic, La Mar Washington.

The trouble with Perdido Isle is that there's so much to explore and so little time to do it. The thought of what might be out there is frustrating for young Gaspar. Now that he and Alex are back from their amazing Christmas vacation in Antarctica, both teenagers look forward to getting back not only to their studies at Andrew Jackson Junior High, but also to all the extracurricular activities that Gaspar and his gang of friends enjoy, including exploring their own backyard!

CHAPTER 1

AN URGENT MESSAGE

I T WAS FINALLY FRIDAY, THE END OF THE FIRST WEEK OF SCHOOL AFTER CHRISTMAS VACATION. GASPAR AND ALEX were goofing off in the cafeteria during their lunch hour when Gaspar's cell phone buzzed. It was Peter Cawthorne, Gaspar's attorney and soon to be stepfather on the line. Peter apologized for interrupting the boys lunch, something interesting had come up and he needed Gaspar to stop by the office after school. This peaked Gaspar's curiosity and he couldn't wait for classes to end so he could hightail it over to Peter's office. The minute the bell rang he grabbed Alex and ran to the old woody station wagon, which stood idling by the sidewalk with La Mar Washington behind the wheel.

"La Mar, we need to go to Peter's office before heading home." Gaspar told the driver, "It'll just take a minute," he promised, "so just wait for us by the curb." He instructed.

The drive to Peter's took less than five minutes, and barely before the car had stopped, the teenagers jumped out and ran inside. Peter was waiting and ushered them into his private inner sanctum.

"Do you mind if Alex joins us?" Gaspar asked, hoping that the business at hand wasn't confidential.

"Oh, not at all, Gaspar. What I have to tell you is not earth-shattering, but I do think it'll be right up your alley." The lawyer hinted, handing his young client a set of rusty, old keys on a ring.

"What are these for?" Gaspar asked, turning the clunky old keys over in his hand before passing them to Alex.

"They arrived this morning, Federal Express from Chicago." Peter filled him in. "It seems that we have a vacant property on our hands. It's the old Sullivan mansion over in Llojeta. I received this letter today from the Sullivans' family attorney. It seems the family no longer has need of their old winter residence on Perdido Isle."

"So what do you have in mind, Peter? I certainly don't need another house … do I? Can't you just put it up for rent or sell it or something?" Gaspar asked quizzically. "If it's a great old house, I'd love to see it. You know how much I enjoy architecture and antiques, but other than that…. What's the catch, Peter?"

"I think there's something more … something I think you like even more than old architecture and antiques." Peter suggested cryptically. "You see, the old Sullivan mansion has another name. The locals have always called it, *The House of Mystery*." Peter filled his young client in, his words hitting Gaspar like a bombshell.

"The House of Mystery, I know where that's at, Mr. Cawthorne Sir." Alex shuddered, "We don't want to go there. Ever since THE TRAGEDY … everyone knows that place is haunted!"

"You've gotta be kidding me." Gaspar shook his head. "A haunted house! What's the address Peter? Count me in … I'm on my way. Yes sir-ee! … that's for me all right." he insisted enthusiastically turning towards the door, grabbing the ring of keys out of Alex's hand.

"Wait a minute, Gasp. You don't know the circumstances yet." Peter stopped the enthusiastic teenager in his tracks. "The house has been abandoned for years and years. The Sullivans' trustees in Chicago and what's left of the Sullivan family are finally just sick of paying for it. Apparently there is a live-in caretaker who's worked for the family for the past 50 years. According to the lawyers letter, they haven't had any physical contact with him in decades. Except for the fact that money is transferred to ·the caretaker's bank account once a month, they've had absolutely no contact from him … not even a word of acknowledgment. The only thing they know for sure is that the bank account is active.

"What's Alex talking about ... what's 'THE TRAGEDY'?" Gaspar mimicked the panic he'd heard in his best friends voice.

It's true, the house was the scene of a tragedy, as Alex has so succinctly pointed out. It happened many years ago. Two brothers, known around here as The Sullivan Twins were holed up in the place, living like recluses, too scared to step outside. They had booby-trapped the house to insure that intruders wouldn't be able to get at them. Apparently in the middle of the night, one of the brothers accidently triggered one of the booby-traps and was crushed to death under a falling mahogany bookcase filled with a mountain of books. The other brother who was an invalid and completely dependent on his twin for his daily upkeep starved to death in his bed, unable to summon help."

"How do you know all this, Peter?"

"That's the official story put out by the police and the United Press at the time There seems to be no other explanation or theory. Why do you ask?" Peter asked suspiciously.

"Oh, I don't know, it just seems so implausible." Gaspar shrugged.

"So who called the police?" Alex asked

"The caretaker." Peter answered

"I was wondering about him." Gaspar looked at the lawyer with disbelief.

"Apparently the servant was never allowed inside the main house. He delivered food through a revolving cupboard in the kitchen. When the food wasn't being taken into the house, he became worried, but he was afraid to call the cops thinking his employers would get mad at him. It was about a month later when he finally worked up the courage to call the authorities. Let's just say, what they found inside the mansion was gruesome." Peter informed his teenaged friends.

"Well, did they disarm all the booby-traps?" Gaspar asked. "Is it safe for us to go inside?" he turned the keys over in the palm of his hand clanking them together.

"I think it's safe. Since it's your property, I thought you'd like to take a look at it and assess the situation. It's a huge parcel of land, an entire square block, and if the house is not habitable, you might like to tear it down, subdivide the land and maybe even build. You can probably get at least ten houses on that land." Peter had on his lawyer, developer, banker, hat now. This is right up your alley, Gasp and yours too, Alex, since you want to grow up to be an architect. Go over and check it out and report back to me. Besides, you'll probably find a lot of old furniture in that place, which I know you're going to want to do something with." Peter held out a carrot that he knew Gaspar couldn't refuse. "Just be careful. Take your time. Be cautious … just in case some of those crazy booby-traps are still in place." He warned the boys as they left the office.

CHAPTER 2

ANOTHER *RUMFUSTIAN* ADVENTURE

WHEN GASPAR AND ALEX HIT THE SIDEWALK THEY
RAN SMACK INTO THEIR PALS, THE ARDEN TWINS.
Kevin and June Arden were two of Gaspar's favorite
classmates and the ones he and Alex liked to hang out
with after school as much as possible.

"Hey guys, *where-ya goin'* in such a hurry?" Kevin
asked.

"We've got a new *Rumfustian* adventure to look into."
Gaspar told them, "Do ya-wanna join us?"

"If it's really a *Rumfustian* adventure," June piped up,
"you can count on us, for sure!"

"Hop in," Alex opened the back door of the waiting
woody. "Let's get moving."

"The Sullivan Mansion in Llojeta." Gaspar instructed La Mar, "Do you know how to find it, La Mar, or do you need the address? They call it, The House of Mystery!" Gaspar added dramatically.

"THE HOUSE OF MYSTERY!" Kevin, June and La Mar all blurted out simultaneously.

"Take us there now La Mar. That's our next stop."

"I jus hope it not be de las stop o de day," La Mar shuddered gripping the steering wheel tightly.

"What do you know that we don't know about The House of Mystery, Kev?" Alex asked his pal.

"You've gotta be kidding," Kevin replied, having regained his composure. "It's the gang's favorite Halloween haunt every year, all tricks … no treats!" he laughed. "Don't you remember last year? We TP'd the place Gasp … you and Al were there."

"Oh yeah, I remember that place … SPOOOOKY! How could I forget that night? I was scared to death the entire time," Gaspar confessed.

"Oh great Gasp, if you were scared on Halloween … you better prepare yourself for a real haunted house … on the inside this time." Alex chuckled.

"If I had known it was that place, I would have brought a change of underwear," Gaspar insisted, laughing.

"Give us a break, Gasp. Everyone knows you don't ever wear any underwear." Alex snorted.

"Not for me Al … I was thinking for you … your acting *sooooo scaaared of the spooooks* all of a sudden," Gaspar laughed at his nervous friend. He also wanted to change the subject as he thought his lack of underwear was probably too much information for June to hear about from a *Ripe-Reeking-Pig-nut* like Alex. "Kev, you seem to be the expert on the subject, tell us everything you know about this supposedly haunted house." Gaspar was all ears.

"Oh boy, you guys don't want to know. There were two brothers, The Sullivan Twins, Tommy and Timmy. The family were big real-estate tycoons from Chicago. Something happened to them back home, something so terrible that they both feared for their lives … and so they moved to their family's holiday house here on Perdido Isle. In those days this island was still a very secluded, out of the way place. They lived in hiding, barricaded inside their house like a couple of animals. My granddaddy knew them and he told me all about them … even took me to visit them one day when I was just a squirt but they wouldn't let us in and only spoke to us through an open window that was eight feet off the ground. I remember that visit as if it were yesterday … but that was before they died so mysteriously." Kevin finished up.

"How'd they die?" June wanted to know, "And why haven't you ever told me about any of this before, and why didn't Grand take me with you?" She asked her twin brother crossly.

"Gee I don't know Sis, I guess Granddaddy probably thought you might not be interested, like when he used to take me fishing. You never wanted to go fishing with us did you?"

"No I never wanted to go fishing with you and Grand, but a haunted house, that's something different." June insisted.

"It's funny … I haven't thought about that visit to the Sullivans with Grand for years." Kevin confessed.

"Sounds spooky," Alex breathed.

"Don't listen to them, Gaspar." June joined the fun, "I'm sure it's a beautiful house, or at least it used to be a long time ago. I can't wait to see the interior, I bet its full of treasure too."

"That's The House of Mystery," Kevin blurted out almost jumping over the seat back while pointing straight ahead over La Mar's shoulder towards the tall fenced-in property in front of them.

Gaspar felt the car jerk and looking left saw La Mar's eyes almost popping out of his head. The street dead ahead was clear of traffic but hearing Kevin's mention of, The House of Mystery had caused a knee jerk reaction in the driver.

"What is it La Mar?" Gaspar asked only slightly amused by La Mar's discomfort.

"It ain't nothin boss," La Mar lied, "I jus hope yous not plannin on visitin insaad-a dat howse …"

"What house, La Mar?"

"Da Howse uv Mystry, boss."

"It says here the address is 2613 Via San Marco in Llojeta," Gaspar read the address on the label attached to the keys Peter had given him.

"Dat be it, boss," La Mar's hands were visibly shaking as they grabbed the steering wheel tightly.

CHAPTER 3

THE HOUSE OF MYSTERY

THE WOODY PULLED UP TO WHAT APPEARED FROM ACROSS THE STREET TO BE AN EMPTY LOT, BUT WAS in fact a parcel of land consisting of an entire square block. Looking through a high, wrought-iron fence the visitors could only see a tangled jungle of tropical plants. Where a front lawn should have been followed by a house … thick, wild, uncared for vegetation had taken over. Gaspar was the first to jump out of the car and run across the street. He climbed up on the low, cut-stone wall and clung to the bars of the fence like a monkey at the zoo. Try as he might, he couldn't see past the tall screen of plants.

Jumping down he ran to the right where tall gates stood chained and tightly padlocked. More plants and rubbish blocked his view onto the property. Gaspar couldn't have been more disappointed. Trying the keys Peter had given him, none worked to open the heavy lock.

"You want to get in?" Kevin asked.

"Yeah, I want to get in. It doesn't even look like there's a house back there. Do you think there's someone still living in this mess?" Gaspar quizzed his pal.

"I don't know Gasp, but I doubt it. Come on, where there's a will, there's a way." Kevin took charge, heading back to the car. "Follow me."

Piling back into the woody, this time with Gaspar, June and Alex in the back while Kevin sat up front riding shotgun next to La Mar. As the car pulled away from the curb, Kevin instructed La Mar to drive down the street and take the next left. Before they knew it, they were driving around the block onto Via Genoa the street right behind Via San Marco where they had just been. When the car reached the middle of the block Kevin instructed La Mar to stop. Jumping out, he opened the back door for his sister and his pals. "This should do it," he told them.

They were at the back entrance to the property. A bronze plaque screwed to the gate post just above a rusting doorbell proclaimed: NO PEDDLERS OR AGENTS NEED RING THIS BELL. The low stone wall and iron fence ringing the entire block was identical to the one they'd climbed on, out in front. The jungle was overgrown everywhere with the exception of the tall service gates leading up a cracked concrete driveway to a tradesmen's entrance entirely paved and devoid of vegetation except for occasional three-foot-tall weeds growing through cracks in the pavement. The gate was duly padlocked and again none of the keys in Gaspar's possession would open it. There was a gap to the left of the gate, where the post had separated from the railing, created an opening that three skinny teenagers might be able to squeeze through. While La Mar pleaded with them to get back in the car, Gaspar shimmied his way through the opening, then helped June through, followed by Alex and finally Kevin.

Creeping up the service driveway, they made their way slowly forward and around a bend. That's when they realized that all was not lost. Before them stood a detached carriage house. On their left a high wall of cut stone was inset with a gate, but unlike the others they'd encountered, this gate was wide open, barely hanging on its rusted hinges. Passing through the gate they discovered a ruined garden, its once formal parterres dried to twigs, and its once beautiful specimen roses, blooming wild and rangy all over the place. There were Italian marble statues of the four continents, and a carved marble fountain filled mostly with dirt and old leaves. Giant trees, badly in need of trimming, cast the entire area in gloomy shade and it wasn't until they were well past these that the house finally revealed itself.

It was a massive Victorian house in the French style. Steep-pitched Mansard roof with turrets and towers that rose high above walls of pink stucco, pierced by tall French windows, and shaded by elegantly colonnaded verandas. The three friends stood speechless at the sight of their discovery.

Gaspar piped up, "Look at the windows, you guys, they're all boarded up … from the inside."

"Yeah, but look over there, Gasp," Kevin pointed, "Look at those shutters, they're nailed shut too, it's just that the shutters on the boarded up windows you're looking at have totally disintegrated.

Stepping closer they saw broken down, weather-beaten garden furniture, scattered hither and thither under the veranda, more lying down than standing on four legs.

"This furniture looks like it's been tossed around by several decades of hurricane gales," June observed mournfully.

"Yeah, and look over there. Check out the ceiling of that porch." Gaspar pointed upwards. "It's falling down and look there," he said. "It's rotted right through to the rafters. You can see daylight right through the roof," he lamented.

The four friends spent the next hour walking around the perimeter of the house, getting as close to it as the tangled garden would allow them. Every time they found a door, Gaspar tried it, hoping one of the keys on his ring might work or that one of the doors might unlock but none of the keys worked and none of the doors opened.

Wandering around what should have been magnificent gardens, they trudged along what was left of garden paths, made of old bricks, opening into areas laid out on axis to the house. These holding arbors, and fountains, a tennis court and an old swimming pool. There were also two smaller houses at both ends of the property that the teenagers assumed were guest houses.

Returning to the main house, they climbed up onto the front porch and attempted to see inside the windows there but to no avail. All of the windows they tried to look through had heavy planks of wood roughly nailed over them. Many of the window panes were missing, and Gaspar could only imagine the state of the interiors considering how much water must have entered through the broken glass over the years.

"What a mess," June sighed, "It's basically in the same condition as the old house we found at The Seminole Spring, Gaspar." She reminded him of that adventure and the wonderful old Queen Anne house they subsequently restored.

"Yeah," Gaspar chuckled, "and when I first showed it to you June, you said it could never be fixed, but look at it now, it's already been published in three different magazines." He gloated. "The only difference between that house and this one is that this one is ten times bigger than the old Queen Anne cottage at The Seminole Spring."

"What're ya thinking Gasp? Do you think you'd want to fix up this old place?" Alex asked.

"I don't know Al, what do you think? From what Peter told us, I guess the tenants have abandoned it, and haven't paid the land lease, so I guess it's mine to do with as I want. Let's see if we can get inside." He said, fumbling with the keys one more time.

"Do you really think you're going to find anything worth saving inside this old ruin?" Kevin laughed. "If I were you I'd just call for the bulldozers."

"I don't know Kev, I'll have to ask Peter again. He knows all the ins and outs of our business around here. Right this minute, I'm more interested in the architecture … but we've got the keys … so let's see if they work the front door at least. I have to admit, I'm curious to see what's inside and of course I'm also interested in the MYSTERY too." Gaspar chuckled. "Here, you try the keys this time, Kev. Maybe you'll have better luck than I've had. I really want to see the rest of it." Gaspar told him, crossing his fingers.

The front door had five different locks on it, and Gaspar had five different keys. One by one Kevin tried them and one by one, through trial and error they eventually opened each of the locks with a loud click. "Good work Kev! That does it!" Gaspar exclaimed, "Follow me!"

With a shriek of rusted hinges he pushed the door open. The house moaned a melancholy warning as the door reluctantly revealed the entrance hall, but none of them heard or heeded it. The light inside the house was dim due to the boarded-up windows and the air which rushed out and enveloped the intruders was stale and sickly sweet. Gaspar tried the light switch but to no avail, the massive crystal chandelier didn't turn on. Pulling out his cell phone he flipped on the flashlight and Alex, Kevin and June followed suit with their own.

"Well that's not much better," Gaspar chuckled nervously, "Let's stick together and use all our flashlights like one so we can see as much as possible, and don't forget, this place may still be booby-trapped, so watch your steps."

Slowly the three teenage sleuths, standing shoulder to shoulder in the middle of the entrance hall, moved their flashlights around the vast, high-ceilinged area. What had once been a grand foyer was littered with trash, old newspapers, and magazines, boxes spilled over with old rags stacked one on top of the other, and even three metal garbage cans that apparently were filled with old phonograph records. The rose pink, flocked wallpaper hung in tatters, and the once polished mahogany staircase, doors and door surrounds were now dull with old, alligatored varnish. There was a carpet underfoot, but it was filthy with grime and felt gritty under their feet.

Silently they entered the room on their right which promised to be a drawing room. What they found there was the remains of a once formal room but again every surface was covered with boxes and stacks of old clothes, broken dishes, and mountains of old clocks of every variety. One sofa was loaded down with old lunch boxes featuring pictures of Howdy Doody, The Flintstones and The Jetsons.

"They were hoarders," June breathed through clenched teeth, holding her handkerchief over her mouth and nose, "What a mess."

"Let's see what's through here," Gaspar suggested, "It's either gotta be a double parlor or a library."

Skirting through the debris they pushed their way into what had been a double parlor, but instead of a room they found several narrow tunnels created by the systematic placement of walls of books, and at least thirteen upright pianos. Added to this improvised architecture were lamps of every shape and size, and boxes of chandelier crystals, and Christmas ornaments. They navigated these corridors single file coming out at the other end where a closed door should have led back into the entrance hall.

"Don't touch that door!" Gaspar warned ... too late ... as Alex pulled the heavy mahogany door open with a mighty heave.

Grabbing Alex by the back of his shirt collar, Gaspar yanked him backwards as the door swung open, accidentally knocking June backwards on her bottom, with a scream. Kevin caught his sister before she hit the floor just as a pile of crystal glasses and other crystal tabletop articles crashed down from the Sullivans' booby-trap above the opened door. Crystal splinters and shards were flying in every direction as the four kids rolled out of harm's way.

After the crashing cacophony and earsplitting explosion of fine crystal hitting mahogany hardwood floors subsided, Alex cursed just like Captain Haddock, the way Gaspar had taught him. "*Billions of Bilious Blue Blistering Barnacles in a Thundering Typhoon!*" he screamed. "Where in the name of *Stinking Blue Dolphins* did that blast come from?" He asked no one in particular

"You tripped a booby-trap, Al. I tried to stop you but I was too late. The Sullivans', *Those Tinfoil-Hatted, Tyrant-Twins*, have struck again!" Gaspar cursed, just like Captain Haddock, his favorite character from *Tin Tin*.

"Of all the ridiculous, *Spur-galled, Shard-borne, Hasty Witted, Folly Fallen, Clack-dish* tricks I've ever heard of! Gasp … I could have been killed!" Alex finally calmed and shuddered, realizing the narrow escape he'd just had. "That was attempted murder, Gasp," he wailed.

"Are you alright, June?" Gaspar inquired, checking on his other two friends. "I'm sorry I knocked you down. I hope I didn't hurt you."

"I'm okay Gaspar, just a little shaken up." June breathed heavily. "That was a near miss, you really dodged that bullet, Alex."

"How bout you, Kev? All in one piece?"

"Yeah, Gasp… but that was a close one. How bout you?"

Just a little cut on my hand," Gaspar said wrapping his handkerchief around his palm. "How bout you Al, any cuts or scrapes?"

"No, I'm fine." Alex insisted.

"No you're not," June told him, pointing her flashlight at his face, "*you're bleeding*!"

Alex reached up and felt the blood on his cheek. "Holy Abalone," he shouted, "Now I can finally tell people that I cut myself shaving."

Everyone laughed. Alex's funny, having broken the ice after their heart pounding scare. June took out her handkerchief and dabbed Alex's cheek with it before handing it over for him to hold.

"Let's get out of here," Gaspar insisted. "This is no place for us to be exploring in the dark. I'm gonna get Peter to turn the lights on and remove all the wood from these windows so we can actually see something. Retracing their steps they locked the front door behind them and headed back through the spooky garden to the service entrance.

"Let's check out the carriage house and see if we can get inside." Gaspar suggested since the building was at hand.

Dutifully, Kevin and Alex ran forward but were unable to budge the enormous barn doors, or pry open the side door which they thought would have led to a staircase and groom's quarters upstairs. Pressing their faces against the window panes was even less satisfying as all of the lower carriage house windows had been covered over with boards as well. That's when June let out a blood-curdling scream, and the three boys rushed back into the center of the motor court where she stood staring upwards.

"What is it June?," Kevin asked throwing his arms around her.

June was as white as a ghost, staring up at the old carriage house with a terrified expression on her face. Slowly she raised her arm and pointed. "I saw someone … something? There's somebody up there … *in the carriage house!*"

"Don't be silly, June," Kevin comforted her, "you're imagining things."

Suddenly, Alex yelped, turned around and ran down the driveway arms flailing and lungs screeching, as he pushed himself through the crack in the fence. Gaspar and Kevin both looked up towards what would have been the groom's quarters and saw what June and Alex had also seen. "Yikes," Kevin yelled, "Let's get out of here!" he hollered grabbing June's hand and dragged her down the driveway with Gaspar in hot pursuit.

Squeezing through the fence, they hightailed it to the Woody, which La Mar had thrown in gear the minute he saw the terror-stricken, blood-smeared.face of Alex heading his way. Safely back in the car, they breathed a sigh of relief as La Mar took off with the scream of pealing rubber, heading for Calaluna.

"It's almost 4:00, time for tea." Gaspar insisted after taking a deep breath. "La Mar, take us to Karen's Café please, I think we all need a drink!" He chuckled, "That means you too La Mar."

"Yes Suh," La Mar shuddered, "Buh whaa Ah wann, Ah doan thinc I's-a-gonna-fine at Karen's Café, Suh. Ah'll be droppin you young folk off at da Karen's and Ah be waitin' on Y'all

CHAPTER 4

A POW WOW AT KAREN'S

KAREN'S CAFÉ WAS PERDIDO ISLE'S VERSION OF THE
CAFÉ DE PARIS IN PARIS, FRANCE. IF YOU SAT THERE
long enough you were bound to see someone you knew
coming through the door. It was where Gaspar and Alex
and their friends liked to hang out at the counter to eat
and dish the dirt. The four friends, and La Mar had
driven in complete silence from The House of Mystery,
too scared to talk about what they'd just seen. They each
spent the half-hour drive to formulate their thoughts. It
wasn't until they were safely seated side by side at the
counter of Karen's Café that they could finally formulate
their words.

"Who the *drivelswiggers* was watching us from that
window Gasp?" Alex finally blurted out. "Did you see him

Gasp? Did you see him Kev? You saw him June. You saw him. It was the … the … it was the Devil!" Alex finally spat out the words and started shaking again.

"I saw him Alex. I saw him, and I thought it was a ghoul or a ghost or … maybe the Devil … I don't know… but I saw something … something horrible … and it moved around … it wasn't just a statue in the window … it was …. ALIVE!" June grabbed her brother's hand almost in tears.

"Gaspar and I both saw it," Kevin insisted. "I don't know what I saw … but I hope I never have to see anything like that again." Kevin shuddered.

"I saw what I think was a man, looking at us from the window." Gaspar was cool calm and collected. "It scared the *scrap* out of me, but this is what I saw. A guy, old, white, wrinkled, no hair on his head, but a wisp of something pointing straight up, a thin pointed nose, big pointed ears, big round black eyes, and thin wide lips … he had on some kind of a shirt, a round collar like a t-shirt, but with wide red and black stripes, and that's all I saw. He didn't smile, he didn't gesture, and he didn't threaten, but he was ugly enough to scare the *Spongy Slubberdegullion Scrap* out of me … that's for sure," he Haddocked.

At that moment, Karen stepped forward with her always-cheerful welcome. "Good afternoon mates. How's it going today and what can I get for you?" Karen greeted her guests while looking around the café, taking note of who needed what. When she finally looked at her pals, she jumped back. *"Holy Heliotrope*, what's with you four. Y'all look like you've seen a ghost or something. Where have you been playing … *the graveyard*?" she chuckled.

"We've just had a weird experience Karen. We'll tell you all about it, but first we need sustenance. What have you got for us?" Gaspar begged hoping it would be delicious.

"Name your poison. Wha-da-ya got in mind? Ya-wanna soup, or sandwich, burgers, sausages, eggs, give me a hint, throw me a bone for the love of *salmagundi*, kids." The short-tempered soup jockey insisted, rolling her eyes while shrugging her shoulders to emphasize that she basically couldn't care less if they starved to death. "Or do you brats just want desert?"

"I'll have a burger, Karen." Alex was first to decide.

"Me too," June chimed in.

"Make that three," Kevin added.

"I'll have the same," Gaspar made it unanimous, "but I want lettuce, and tomato."

"Me too," Alex agreed, "but add a slice of raw onion to mine, and some cheese too."

"The same for me, Karen. Just combine Gaspar's and Alex's and it'll be perfect." June insisted.

"Same for me," Kevin agreed, but add in bacon and all the rest, please."

"Let's make this simple, Karen. Add it all together and we'll all have the same, lettuce, tomato, onion, cheese and bacon, but keep the ketchup, mustard and mayonnaise on the side. Okay?" Gaspar always had the last word especially since he'd be the one picking up the tab. "Go on Karen, let's hear it," he insisted with a big grin.

The old gal dutifully turned her head and shouted over her shoulder, to Frank, her long suffering short order cook, "Frank, we've got a bridge party here," referring to anything ordered that was four of a kind. "Walk four cows past the stove, then drag them through the garden, pin a rose on them and make them cry." She looked back at Gaspar and his pals and smiled mischievously. "And Frank, don't turn them into hockey pucks, they like them cooked medium and while you're at it, drag them through Wisconsin too." She added letting him know that cheeseburgers had been ordered.

"Bacon Karen, don't forget the bacon!" Gaspar hissed at her urgently.

"Oh yeah, Frank, I almost forgot. Cremate some bacon and throw it on top."

"How bout some Bronx vanilla to top it off?" Frank asked her innocently through the pass through.

"If they wanted halitosis, they would have asked for Italian garlic, your suggestions aren't needed or asked for, Frank." Karen shut him down in no uncertain terms. "Bronx vanilla," she scoffed under her breath. "How about drinks?"

"I'll have an Atlanta special," Alex answered, hoping that was what Karen was calling Coke this afternoon.

"Make mine a Hoboken special," Kevin said, referring to his favorite pineapple soda with chocolate ice cream.

"Oh gross," his sister June choked, "how can you drink that combo." She gagged. "Ever since he was a kid, he's always ordered that disgusting drink ... just to gross me out. I'll have some moo juice please, Karen," she told the waitress, hoping for a plain old glass of milk.

"I'll have a fifty-five, or better yet, put some chocolate ice cream in it and make me one of your famous Black Cow's, Karen. Root beer and chocolate ice cream, my two most favorite ingredients." Gaspar licked his lips. "I need that kind of a pick up after what we've just been through," he insisted.

After Karen suitably yelled the drink orders to Frank she leaned against the counter and asked, "What's all the excitement kids, what is it that's gotten you four into such a lather?"

"Have you ever heard of The House of Mystery?" Gaspar asked breathlessly.

"Are you talking about the old Sullivan mansion out in Llojeta?" she asked wide eyed.

"Yeah, that's the place," Alex answered with a shudder, "Wha-da-ya know about it?"

"Well when I was growing up, the Sullivan Twins were famous, of course they were old way back then, and crazy too. When we were your age, me and my school mates used to go over there and play pranks on the old boys, and of course for Halloween, that was our idea of a real haunted house." Karen remembered the good old days with a sparkle in her eyes and a toothy smile.

"But what can you tell us about the brothers," June probed, "Did you ever see or meet them?"

Karen looked as if she were deep in thought as she turned around and grabbed the drinks Frank laid out on the pass through. "Let me see," she started as she placed the drinks in front of her pals. "If I remember correctly, and these were stories I picked up from my Mom and dad a million years ago, the Sullivans' parents were rich, from Chicago I think, and kind-a reclusive too. They didn't always used to be reclusive, in fact my Mom told me they were bon-vivants, you know, life of the party types. Their Granddaddy was considered a lady killer, what my mother called, 'a man about town'. Then something happened, and the family stopped coming to Perdido Isle for the season … but years later, their kid moved in during the winter months with his wife and twin boys. After the twins' parents died, the two boys moved in permanently, you know, year-round and rarely ever left the house. I haven't thought about the Sullivan twins in a long time," Karen mused. "In fact, I haven't even passed that old house in ages. When I was your age, I used to think it was the most beautiful house in Llojeta." Karen mused wistfully.

"It may have been, Karen," June agreed with her, "but it's derelict now. You can't even see it from the street because the garden's become a veritable jungle. Most of the windows are boarded up and the entire place is just a falling down ruin."

"What crawled over your livers to bring the Sullivan mansion to your attention in the first place?" Karen was becoming fascinated by the turn of events.

"It's just been given back to me..." Gaspar blurted. Apparently, the Sullivan family don't want it anymore and their lawyers have stopped paying the land lease. Since they've abandoned it, I guess it's mine to do whatever I want with it." Gaspar confessed sheepishly.

"What about the TRAGEDY? You do know about the TRAGEDY?" Karen was aching to tell them about the tragedy.

"The TRAGEDY!" all four teenagers blurted at once, "what tragedy?" Looking back and forth at each other they started to giggle for the first time since they'd run away from that terrifying specter in the window. The chill of their morning adventure was quickly evaporating.

"When one of the brothers was killed." Karen said nonchalantly.

"Yes Karen, we know, we're just having some fun with you." Gaspar smiled. "But Karen, are we talking murder?" Gaspar asked, "or was the brothers death accidental?"

"Well if I remember correctly, it was supposed to be a tragic accident, but maybe the police would know better. It was one of the brothers, I can't remember which one. They were twins, one was called Tommy and the other was Timmy. I'm not even sure their own parents could tell them apart." Karen joked, "Anyway, they were scared to death of something, and had barricaded themselves inside the house. The whole place was supposed to be booby trapped and I guess one of them got up in the middle of the night and tripped a wire or whatever and the poor old boy was crushed to death under a mountain of books and falling lumber ... at least that's what I remember, but don't hold it against me if I'm wrong. It's been a long time." Karen gave herself an out ... besides, lunch was waiting on the pass through. "Here's your grub mates," she sang as she unceremoniously plopped, The Works, in front of them.

"Where's the ketchup, Karen?" Gaspar insisted, I want to paint my hockey puck red," he laughed.

"Here's the hemorrhage, and some yellow paint too." Karen was one step ahead of him.

"Anyone else want to Firehouse this like I do?" Alex asked no-one in particular.

"Chili sauce!" on top of all this?" June asked incredulously. "Good idea, shall we make it four?"

"Bring on the chili, Karen, this is going to be a four-alarm lunch." Kevin winked at his sister.

"When you're done eatin' this mess, I'm afraid you're gonna need a shot of the old blue bottle." Karen told them.

"What's the old blue bottle?" Alex asked innocently.

"Bromo Seltzer, you idiot," Gaspar yelled, knocking his shoulder against his best pals.

"That's so crazy that you know about Bromo Selzer Gasp." Kevin marveled, "They stopped making that tonic back in the 1960s. I only know about it cause my Mom used to go to school with a girl she still refers to as The Bromo Seltzer Heiress.

"Yeah, well you know I live on old movies so I'm always picking up a lot of that kind of useless trivia," Gaspar confessed without embarrassment.

"Karen, I'm gonna need some sea dust for these frog sticks." Alex complained, "Frank forgot the salt and you know that's the best part of any French fry."

Sea dust delivered, and mouths full, the four hungry friends let Karen tell them a little more about their quest while they wolfed down their hearty repast. "It was the talk of the town, and there was an inquest and I remember something about an Indian servant, not a Seminole Indian mind you. I mean a towel-head, you know, one of those foreign devils… A HINDI!" Karen smiled at her new-found ability to speak a foreign language.

"I think you mean a Hindu?" June corrected her.

"Holy cow!" Gaspar and June were talking over each other. "A real Indian from India, maybe he was a Hindu mystic, did you ever see him Karen? Did he wear native costume, Khurta pajama's in pink silk embroidered with gold set with stones?" Gaspar was filled with visions of grandeur based on wishful thinking. "Tell us about his turban was it a big turban with feathers and a jeweled brooch or did he wear it close to his head with a long streamer down the back?" Gaspar knew that Karen was anything but politically correct and tried to soften her memory of 'the towel headed, foreign devil' by injecting his own hopeful take on the subject.

"Gaspar, you've gotta be joking, you expect me to remember unimportant details like that?" Karen objected, "Let's just stick to what I do remember, and if you go to the morgue at the Perdido Daily News, you'll probably find pictures of *The White Boned Demon* I'm talking about. How bout some desert kiddies?" she asked seeing that all four of the ravenous teenagers had cleaned their plates.

"May I have rice pudding please," June ordered politely, "and could you put some chocolate syrup on it for me, Karen?"

"Frank, we've got a Chinese here, Ice the Rice and throw some mud on it." Karen screamed in the direction of the pass through.

"I'd like a slice of apple pie, please. And put some cheese on top, okay, Karen?" Kevin begged.

"Frank, a plate of Eve with a moldy lid on it."

"Peach Pie," was Alex's order.

"And some Georgia on a plate, Frank."

Gaspar knew most of Karen's lingo, and ordered "a Houseboat and a slice of raisin cake."

"Frank, Gaspar wants a Dagwood Special and a slice of Roach cake too."

"No Karen, I want a banana split!" Gaspar knew that a Houseboat was the same as a banana split back where Karen came from. "What's a Dagwood Special?"

"Just another name for a Houseboat, Gaspar. I just like to keep you on your toes whenever you're here." the old girl responded with a twinkle in her eye for her favorite customer.

While they devoured their gooey-sweet deserts, Karen finished her recollections of the Sullivan Twins. "Like I told you, they never left the house and had all their provisions brought in from the Italian grocers in Llojeta, and all their bills were paid by accountants or lawyers in Chicago. After the brother was crushed to death, I guess it only took a matter of days for his twin who was an invalid to starve to death in his bed. I don't know what happened to the foreign servant, you know, the towel-head HINDU critter." she drawled looking at June for approval. "I suppose you kids still play pranks on the Sullivan house at Halloween, although I haven't heard of any mischief worth repeating lately.

It was late by the time Gaspar and his pals left Karen's.

"I'm stuffed, Alex, complained.

"Me too," insisted Kevin

"All I want is to go to sleep," June confessed, it's been quite a day.

"We'll drop you and Kevin off, before Al and I head back to La Rinconada. Something tells me that when I get there, I'll want to go straight to sleep too," Gaspar lied.

CHAPTER 5

THE LOVE BIRDS WANT A NEW NEST

WHEN HE GOT HOME, GASPAR FOUND HIS MOTHER AND PETER CAWTHORNE SITTING AT THE DINING room table, just finishing dinner. Gaspar sat down with them in hopes of talking about the old Sullivan mansion. Before he could get a word out, his mother made an announcement not only to his surprise, but to the surprise of her fiancé, Peter Cawthorne as well.

"Gaspar darling," Elvira cooed across the table at her son, I've been thinking, and if you don't mind, I thought I might move into the house in town. You know, the little house in Calaluna." His mother spoke hesitantly, her tone of voice almost asking rather than telling her son, her plan.

"Great idea Mom," Gaspar was delighted, "It's a great house, and you can do it up anyway you like. I'll call my favorite designers at the Duquette Studio in L.A. and tell them to get out here and pull it together for you." The possibilities were so endless that Gaspar always loved the idea of redecorating.

"You won't mind leaving La Rinconada?" his mother asked sweetly.

The idea had never occurred to him, and Gaspar's reaction was not in the least bit uncertain considering he was only a teenager. "I'm not leaving La Rinconada," Gaspar made himself quite clear, "If you want a place of your own Ma, a honeymoon house for after you and Peter are married, it makes a lot of sense to me. I perfectly understand your desire for a house of your very own, but I'm staying here." His statement was made without the slightest emotion or thought that what he might be saying wouldn't be acceptable to his parent.

"Oh," was all that came out of his mother's pretty rosebud pink mouth. "Okay darling, that won't be a problem, whatever you want. I'm sure that Angela and Felix will be able to help you here with anything you might need." Elvira was a little taken aback, and a little confused but she knew that Gaspar for all his youth and inexperience was nothing if not self-sufficient, reliable, and responsible, and that leaving him alone in the huge, treasure-filled house, was no big deal. "I guess that's settled then," was her last word on the subject.

"So Ma, what are your plans for the new house?" Gaspar asked with genuine enthusiasm.

"Plans? Oh I have no plans, I like it just the way it is, I guess cousin Eugenia and I just have the same taste, kinda like you and Uncle Charles it seems."

Gaspar found it amusing that his mother was so easy to please. "What do you think, Peter?" Gaspar asked his lawyer and future stepfather.

"Whatever makes your mother happy, makes me happy, Gaspar. After the wedding, I may want to make a study for myself upstairs, but all in all, it's a very comfortable house, and very convenient to the office too. You're sure you won't be too lonely rambling around in this big old fire trap." He chuckled spreading out his hands, motioning to the massive house all around them.

"Not at all Peter, and besides, you'll be coming here all the time, and I'll be in town all the time too. I think it's a brilliant idea. I've always thought that it was a terrible waste, Cousin Eugenia's beautiful townhouse just sitting there forlorn and empty." Gaspar was on board with the plan.

"I got the idea from you Gaspar," Elvira informed him, "When you took over Villa Gaspar as your club house, I got to thinking, Villa Eugenia, was really more my style than La Rinconada could ever be."

"I understand completely Ma, and approve wholeheartedly." Gaspar put her fears to rest.

"Are you sure you won't be too lonely out here all by yourself, I mean, you're not even old enough to drive yet Gasp." Peter was already feeling guilty of child neglect.

"Don't be absurd Peter. There's no difference between me and the Lygon kids whose father was the Earl of Beauchamp at Madresfield Court in England.

"The who, the what?" Peter had never heard of the Lygon family or their ancestral house, Madresfield Court.

"Their father moved to his Palazzo in Venice and their mother moved to London leaving three teenage kids alone in the historic house with a staff of servants to run amuck with! I'm kinda looking forward to running amuck!" Gaspar joked as he knew, that they knew, it wasn't in his nature to ever be out of control.

"Where did you hear about these people?" Elvira asked completely confounded.

"It's a great book, I found it in Uncle Charlie's library. You guys should read it. It's a page turner all about the actual family that Evelyn Waugh used as his inspiration for *Brideshead Revisited*." Gaspar explained enthusiastically.

"Speaking of historic English country houses and palazzos," Peter changed the subject, "What did you discover at the old Sullivan mansion today?"

"Peter, it's a disaster area. There's no electricity, and the windows are all boarded over, and Alex was nearly killed when he triggered a booby trap that let down an avalanche of about a million Baccarat crystal goblets on his head. I pulled him out of the way just in time so it didn't hurt him, but he could have been a goner! Let's just say it was a close call." Gaspar made himself clear.

"Yikes, I had no idea that I was putting you and Alex in harm's way, I'm sorry Gaspar. What can I do?" Peter asked, distressed.

"What we need to do as soon as possible, Peter, is get the lights turned on and the boards taken away from the windows so we can actually see what we have there. A large 40-foot dumpster would be a good idea too. Those Sullivans' were hoarders! You've never seen such a mess of trash inside a house before! By the way, Peter, I think there's someone living in the carriage house. We'll have to look into that too. It must be a squatter."

"A squatter. That doesn't sound like a good idea." Peter shook his head. "What next?" he wondered aloud.

"Maybe you could charge him rent and let him stay?" Gaspar's Mom, made a sweetly ridiculous suggestion.

"I don't know about that Mom." Gaspar wanted to let her down gently. "I got a good look at the dude and let me tell you something … I don't think he's the rent paying kind, if you get my drift." Gaspar made his feelings known by giving Peter a knowing look and then excused himself saying he needed to take a bath before going to bed. "I feel really dirty having been in that house. In fact, I think that house may require a hazmat team before we're through, Peter."

Those were his last words on the subject before saying goodnight and giving his Mom a kiss.

Chapter 6

Uncle Charlie's Two Cents

Gaspar headed straight to the blue marble bathroom that adjoined the Captain's cabin and started running his bath. It had been a day and a half, and what he wanted tonight was a relaxing soak before going to bed. Besides, he felt gross after scrounging around amidst all the rotting trash in the old Sullivan place. As the steaming hot water filled the carved marble shell and spilled over into the immense carved marble tub he stripped off his clothes and grabbed a bottle of bath salts, dumping a liberal amount into the tub. He watched the suds glisten on top of the water as the bubbles quickly rose to the top. Stepping into the tub, he closed his eyes and allowed his body to completely relax in the hot, rose-scented water.

"So you're going to be on your own?" the booming voice of Uncle Charlie exclaimed.

Gaspar didn't jump or move a muscle, Uncle Charlie's constant intrusions into his private world used to drive him crazy, but not anymore. He realized the best way to combat Charlie's insensitivity was to ignore him as much as possible and to never let him know that the old ghost had gotten under his skin.

"Hi Uncle," Gaspar greeted the well-dressed ghost without opening his eyes. "Yeah, pretty cool huh. We're gonna have this old place all to ourselves very soon, you and I!" Gaspar was beside himself with anticipation but wasn't going to show a lot of enthusiasm right this minute.

"Pretty modern of your mother to cut the apron strings and let you loose like this," Charlie insisted.

"Apron strings, don't be silly. I've never been tied to her apron strings. Get real man," Gaspar insisted opening his right eye and arching his eyebrow. "Besides, I'm not so sure you didn't put the idea into her head in the first place?" Gaspar, opened both eyes to better see the mischievous ghosts reaction to his accusation.

"YOU, accuse ME, of mental shenanigans with your MOTHER? For shame Gaspar, for shame." His Uncle chided him with a chuckle. "By the way … what's the first order of business the minute she moves out?" He asked, just like a school boy, rubbing the palms of his hands together with a toothy grin spread across his face.

"Well, I don't foresee very much changing around here." Gaspar sat up in the bath, moving his eyes left and right, realizing that he hadn't given the idea of living alone at La Rinconada any thought at all. "You and I have always had our way at La Rinconada, Uncle. I guess it will just be more of the same, but even more … much more! You know what you always say Uncle, *More Is More.*" Gaspar chuckled. "I think it's time I take over the black and white room next door, and I guess I'll ask Al if he'd like to move-in permanently. He could have the green room next to the office." Gaspar voiced his thoughts out loud for the first time. "So what have you been up to Uncle Charlie? I've missed talking with you since leaving for Buenos Aires. I missed being with you while I was down south. What have you been up to? By the way, you would have loved Antarctica, Uncle." Gaspar insisted.

"You sure know how to find trouble, Gasp." Uncle Charlie shook his head woefully.

"Find trouble Uncle? I don't go looking for it, it finds me." Gaspar complained, "But I must say, I do like adventure.

"Just like me Gasp, you're a chip off the old block. What's next on your agenda?"

"We have a new real estate situation here. The old Sullivan mansion's been abandoned and Peter's thrown the decision of what to do with it into my lap." Gaspar pretended to complain. "It's kind of a mysterious place, Uncle. It probably has an amazing history … and I intend to find out as much about the Sullivans' and their house as I possibly can."

"I could help you tremendously with that history, Gasp, but I promise I won't unless you get stumped or really beg me for assistance. As you know, from the time when I forced you to solve *The Mystery of the Gasparilla Succession* and find Gasparilla's treasure all on your own, that I've always thought it best for you to find things out for yourself, at least as much as possible. It builds character, that's what old Doctor Mendoza y Mendoza used to tell me whenever I asked him for help and that was way back when I was only just a little older than you are now." Uncle Charlie remembered the good old days.

"Don't give it a second thought, Uncle. I can handle it. But I'll be wanting to ask you a lot of personal recollections, so be prepared to unload some real doozies on me!" Gaspar chuckled as he grabbed the soap and started lathering up.

"So what are your plans for this evening?" Uncle Charlie asked nonchalantly.

"My plans, I have no plans. I'm going to bed. What are your plans?" Gaspar asked the peripatetic ghost.

"Oh, I don't know, perhaps I'll go and see a movie."

"A movie, dressed like that." Gaspar laughed.

"Dressed like what?"

"Like Adolph Manjou in *Stage Door*." Gaspar laughed again as he started shampooing his hair.

"And what would you suggest I wear to the premier of the new Douglas Loehman, Carol Bradie film?"

"Douglas Loehman! Carol Bradie? Are you joshing me? You've been invited to the opening of *Suddenly September*. That's awesome, how'd you rate that? Who-da-ya-know in Hollywood?" Gaspar asked grabbing the hand-held shower and standing up while sputtering out his words as he rinsed the shampoo out of his hair and the soap suds off of his body. "I can't believe it, *Suddenly September*, I'm so jealous, can you bring a friend, can you take me with you? I can't believe you didn't have me invited too!" Gaspar sputtered through the suds.

"Don't get your knickers in a twist, Gasp, not that your wearing any," Uncle Charlie observed. "When you're as old and dead as I am you don't need an invitation, you just go and sit in the best seat in the house and hope the person sitting in your lap turns out to be a pretty girl." Uncle Charlie informed him as he departed through the wall with a flick of his wrist. "By the way, you've still got soap in your left ear." Were the last words Gaspar heard as Charlie's voice trailed away.`

Gaspar relaxed the minute Charlie disappeared. "What a character," he said to himself, as he toweled off and walked into the Captain's cabin, ready for bed. It had been a long day and he wanted to get an early start in the morning. There was a lot of stuff he had to get done before school resumed again on Monday.

CHAPTER 7

UNCLE CHARLIE SPILLS THE BEANS

GASPAR HAD NO INTENTION OF SLEEPING IN ... THE ONLY THING HE WANTED TO DO THIS SATURDAY morning was to get to the bottom of the Sullivan twins and the mysterious secret of their old house. For that, he wanted to consult with Uncle Charlie, and also spend some time going through his library hoping to find some clues in Charlies' scrap books of old newspaper clippings. He knew he wouldn't be disturbed by Alex this morning, as Alex always slept in on Saturdays.

"Uncle Charlie," Gaspar called as he pulled several bound volumes from the shelves, "Uncle Charlie, are you here?"

"Present and accounted for, a voice boomed from high up on the balcony. Where's the fire?" Uncle Charlie asked, nonplussed.

"Come on down, Uncle. I need some help here." Gaspar begged.

Charlie jumped over the railing and floated to the ground landing softly on his shiny patent leather clad feet. "What kind of help ... are you in big trouble or just curious about the movie last night?"

"Well of course I want to hear about the premier, and the party afterwards, but please try not to make me any more jealous than I already am." Gaspar begged him.

"I'll make it simple for you, Gasp. The movie is a bomb, who wants to see a show about rich people, who lose all their money and turn their house into a bed and breakfast for illegal aliens?" Uncle Charlie guffawed. "I haven't anything good to say about it, but the party was fantastic. Shall I tell you about Carol Bradie, or have you got the picture?"

"I think I've heard enough Uncle. I still wish I could have gone with you."

"Next time, I promise, I'll get you invited, and I promise not to ruin the picture for you, now stop sulking and tell me how I can help you this glorious morning when you should be outside, surfing, or swimming, or sailing.

"I don't have time for any of that right now. I'm obsessed with the Sullivans', Uncle and want to get to the bottom of how their property became so derelict. When I was there yesterday with Al and June and Kevin we couldn't believe what a mess it is! Basically it's a falling down ruin ... but not deserted ... I saw someone, or something, through the window ... in the room over the carriage house." Gaspar blurted as he furiously turned the pages of the scrapbook hoping for insight."

"Hold everything Gasp," Uncle Charlie sat down across from his mortal nephew. "Close the scrapbook and tell me what you want to know. Perhaps I can help you."

Gaspar did as he was told before asking, "Who were they? The Sullivans, tell me about the family, and Uncle, don't leave anything out."

"Well, let me see. That's a rather tall order ... I guess the only thing to do is to start at the beginning ... and that's going back a long, long time ... but if you insist ... here goes." Uncle Charlie took a deep breath. "Let's see, The Sullivans, were one of the most eccentric families in America. The great-grandparents were the first to build in Llojeta way back in the 1920s when I started developing the town. They were rich, but that goes without saying ... you've seen the house ... and a full square block of land, a full acre. Well, the old boy affected a title, he called himself Sir George Sullivan. Maybe he came from Ireland, or England, nobody ever bothered to find out, and maybe the title was real, or maybe it was just put on.... Who cares? If he wanted to be called Sir George, it mattered not to us in the 1920s." Uncle Charlie chuckled.

"Needless to say, George Sullivan was an unusual man and that's putting it mildly. A lot of people around here thought he was a madman or possibly a joker, especially since his most notable gift to humanity was the invention of a small pistol for shooting wasps."

"Wasps?" Gaspar was incredulous.

"Yeah, and when he was testing it out, he managed to shoot his gardener in the behind, or derriere, or backside, whatever you want to call it." Charlie chuckled. "The man was up on a ladder when George accidently shot him. When he fell off the ladder he knocked a wasp nest off one of the rafters and was severely stung while Sir George barricaded himself inside the house. Talk about adding insult to injury!" Uncle Charlie laughed again.

"Wasps, that's hysterical Uncle Charlie. Did the gardener sue or die or anything?

"Gaspar, gardeners didn't sue in the 1920s, nobody did … but we're getting off the subject. I can assure you that George Sullivan was neither crazy nor a joker, he was just an eccentric with a lot of time on his hands, that's all." Uncle Charlie smiled and shrugged. "Sir George insisted that he enjoyed a large and reliable income from his estates, which he claimed covered 50-square miles of the northern tip of some underappreciated county somewhere in Northern Minnesota. I like to think that the greatest achievement of his unremarkable life was the building of Sullivan Hall, right here on Perdido Isle. A more beautiful estate would be hard to find anywhere in the world, Gasp, except right here at La Rinconada of course." Uncle Charlie patted himself on the back.

"Well you should see Sullivan Hall now, Uncle, it's a derelict ruin." Gaspar interjected.

Without acknowledging Gaspar's comment Uncle Charlie continued not missing a beat to his narrative. "He also wrote and published one noteworthy book, and fathered a son, Edward Carrol Sullivan. For the rest of his time on earth, he tried to find something to do to fill his days and he recorded his efforts meticulously. If we could get into that library, there's no telling what amazing accounts we might discover there." Uncle Charlie enthused. I remember attending a séance at his house with the celebrated medium Madame Florence. I can't remember exactly who we were trying to get in touch with but it was someone interesting like my old friend, Mata Hari, if I remember correctly.

"You knew Mata Hari?" Gaspar was impressed.

"Of course I knew Mata, now don't interrupt me, Gaspar. As I was saying … Everything was going swimmingly until Sir George noticed what appeared to be a set of corset stays beneath the ethereal veil of the manifest spirit of Mata Hari, so naturally he grabbed hold of her and pinned her down until the lights came on. Sir George was not surprised to discover that he was holding onto Madam Florence, clad only in her underwear, but everyone else present including myself was somewhat startled when we saw the *Squawking Popinjay* in the all-together." He chuckled at the memory of the charlatan seeress Madame Florence.

"The *Mammering Misconstrued Mountebank*!" Gaspar Captain Haddocked for Uncle Charlie's delectation while keeping an exaggerated look of outrage on his face.

"Yes, it's true," Uncle Charlie confirmed Gaspar's facetious reaction. "Believe it or not, Gasp, Sir George actually ran for the Senate in 1926 and won a Senate seat for Minnesota. After four years, spending as little time in Washington as possible, it was reported that he'd only asked a total of eight questions during his entire political career. If I remember correctly one of his questions was to the then Attorney General. If you can believe it, he actually asked, 'If it were feasible for the United States to annex the Republic of Bolivia as the 49th state in the union.' Needless to say the Majority Leader, Charles Curtis abstained from answering, to the delight of the entire chamber." Uncle Charlie guffawed heartily.

"Tell me about his wife, Uncle." Gaspar asked. Was she as eccentric as he was?"

"Lady Ida Carrol? Well, she never used the title, and was very down to earth, but nutty as a fruitcake." Uncle Charlie assured him. "Sir George told everyone that his wife was the daughter of the Second Baron Boroughmarsh. To put it mildly, the lady was profligate, if you know what I mean?"

Gaspar shook his head in the negative.

"You know, utterly and shamelessly immoral, completely dissipated and thoroughly dissolute and just to add insult to injury, Gaspar, the woman was also recklessly prodigal with her husband's money … get the picture? We're talking… EXTRAVAGANT." Uncle Charlie made it clear to Gaspar what he meant by the word, 'profligate'.

"She sounds a little bit like you, Uncle Charlie." Gaspar joked.

"Watch it kid, you're treading on thin ice. Do you want me to continue or don't you?" Uncle Charlie joked back.

"Please continue," Gaspar yawned.

"Okay, To be honest, as far as I could tell, their marriage was grounded in mutual indifference from an early stage, but they did have a son nonetheless. John Singer Sargent painted an unhappy group portrait of the three Sullivans around 1925. They used to brag that it was the last portrait Sargent ever painted."

"I wonder if that portrait's still hanging at Sullivan Hall?"

"Try looking over the fireplace in the library," Uncle Charlie suggested. "That's where they used to display it. It was around 1930 if I remember correctly that Sir George's propensity for the bizarre reached another level. It was after Sir George left Washington, he made headlines when he refused to pay off Lady Ida's many creditors. He actually watched in court as she was prosecuted and imprisoned for three years. While she was in jail, he took the opportunity to divorce her and then took their ten-year-old son, Edward to live in Bolivia. Through a series of finally successful lawsuits, Ida got half of George's vast fortune and was ultimately able to pay her debts and get out of jail. She also got the house here on Perdido Isle and lived there in style until her death ten years later. She never saw her son again, and some say she died of a broken heart. Try as she may to spend every penny she could lay her hands on to support her ultra-luxurious lifestyle, she still died a very rich but lonely woman. Even she who was a professional spendthrift couldn't spend it all. When they settled her estate, I read in the paper that whatever was left of her half of Sir George's fortune she'd placed in trust for her only son Edward.

"Sounds like there still must be a huge fortune somewhere if the tax man hasn't taken it all, Uncle." Gaspar figured.

Trust me Gasp, there was plenty to go around, you have to remember, it was all made before the invention of income tax too! Believe me boy, those were the days when you could keep the money you made or in my case the money you found, and spend it as you pleased. I don't see how people today can survive with the government forever picking their pockets to fund projects that mean nothing to the people who are paying for them through hard work?" Uncle Charlie shook his head woefully.

"I agree with you about the evils of Income Tax Uncle, but for now…let's concentrate on the Sullivans." Gaspar wanted to get back to the chase.

"With his half of the scudi, Sir George purchased a large ruined castle inhabited by a family of twenty five squatting Aymara Indians, located deep in the Yungas Valley, which was about an hour's drive outside of La Paz, Bolivia. I went to visit him there once, and believe me, after he fixed it up, it became a world-renowned showcase. The road ran along the property for five miles and there were seven waterfalls and a river where Sir George built his own hydroelectric plant. He named his Castle "El Chaco" and over the next decade restored it to its original Spanish Colonial splendor. He and his son Edward took up permanent residence there, writing repeatedly to President Roosevelt and Henry Morgenthau Jr, Roosevelts Secretary of the Treasury to explain that illegal income taxes had forced him to settle permanently in Bolivia."

"Woo-Wee," Gaspar whistled. "What a story, tell me more Uncle."

"Well this is the best part of all," Uncle Charlie promised. "While living high on the hog in the Bolivian jungle, and with three hundred more peasants at his beck and call, living in the neighborhood, Sir George decided to anoint himself, George the First, Emperor of Bolivia!"

"Oh no Uncle," Gaspar shrieked, clapping his hands with delight … you've gotta be kidding."

"Not at all, it's well documented," Uncle Charlie insisted, "look it up. Anyway, His self-proclaimed Imperial Majesty, Emperor George I, was a celebrated citizen of Bolivia who subsequently added the title Protector of Alto Peru and Knight of the Holy Roman Empire onto his moniker. There were subsequent rumors that he had lost a portion of his vast fortune speculating in Peruvian Rice, but I have firsthand knowledge that there was no truth to that story."

"What really happened, Uncle? About the rice that is … I want to know." Gaspar insisted.

"It was all just business as usual. Sullivan thought he saw a business opportunity when someone told him that China was facing a severe famine and had placed a ban on the export of rice. The ban caused the price of rice in the United States to skyrocket from four cents per pound to thirty-six cents per pound. When he heard that the freighter *Glyde*, was leaving Peru for the United States, carrying 200,000 pounds of rice, he bought the entire shipment for twelve and a half cents per pound thinking he'd cornered the market. Shortly after he signed the contract, several other shiploads of rice left Peru for California causing the price of rice to plummet to three cents a pound. Sullivan tried to void the contract, stating that the dealer had misled him as to the quality of the rice he had contracted for. For the next four years, Sullivan and the rice dealers were involved in protracted litigation. Although Sir George prevailed in the lower courts, the case later reached both the Bolivian and the Peruvian Supreme Courts which ruled against Emperor George. In order to avoid paying his debt, he declared bankruptcy in America and retreated to his castle in the jungle for several years. Of course his actual fortune had been transferred to a secret, numbered account in Switzerland long before he'd ever moved to Bolivia."

"So he never really went broke, Uncle?" The story was getting so convoluted that Gaspar needed confirmation.

"Oh no, not at all, he was loaded, Sullivan was never broke, not in the least, not ever!"

"Did he ever come out of seclusion, Uncle?"

"Oh, yes ... eventually, and when he did, he came back with a vengeance, as The Emperor of course. He was forever interrupting business in the Bolivian Congress and although he had no political power, his influence extending only so far as he was humored by those around him. He was treated deferentially in the halls of government in La Paz, and even the currency he issued in his name was honored in the establishments he frequented."

"He printed his own currency?" Gaspar was dumbfounded.

"Oh yes, of course, and why not? He was the Emperor." Uncle Charlie chuckled before continuing. "He was considered insane, or at least highly eccentric, the citizens of La Paz celebrated his regal presence and his Imperial proclamations with gusto. In his self-appointed role of Emperor, Sullivan issued numerous decrees on matters of state. After having assumed absolute control over the Republic, at least in his own mind, he saw no further need for a legislature, and on October 12, 1859, he issued a decree formally abolishing the Bolivian Congress. In it, Emperor George I insisted that 'fraud and corruption were preventing a fair and proper expression of the public voice.' He went on to express his fear that 'open violation of the laws in Bolivia were constantly occurring, caused by the undue influence of political mobs, parties, factions and sects.' Because of what he saw, He brought the political corruption in the halls of Congress to the people's attention, pointing out that, 'they were not enjoying the protection of person and property which they were entitled to under the Bolivian Constitution.' In order to drain the government swamp he ordered all interested parties to assemble at The Teatro Mignon in La Paz to 'remedy the evil complained of, through demonstrations, boycotts and non-violent labor strikes.' At the assembly, Sullivan issued an Imperial Decree ordering the Army to depose the elected officials of the Bolivian Congress. His rally cry was so successful that the people rose up and shut down the city for over a week until the government finally resigned. Look through that album, Gaspar." Uncle Charlie told him motioning to one of the large leather bound binders that Gaspar had taken off the shelf. "Somewhere in there you'll find a press clipping about all of this." Uncle Charlie said, as Gaspar rummaged through the many pages of clipped newspaper articles.

"Here it is … look." Gaspar shouted, holding the open page with a clipping from the Bolivian newspaper *El Diaro*, up for Charlie to see. "I'll read it to you, Uncle. 'WHEREAS, a body of men calling themselves the National Congress are now in session in our capital, La Paz, in violation of our Imperial Edict of the 12th of October last, I, George I, Emperor of Bolivia, Protector of Alto Peru and Knight of the Holy Roman Empire hereby declare that said Congress be abolished; I hereby order my Imperial Army to disband the brigands and bring order to my government.'"

"Ha ha ha … see I wasn't kidding," Uncle Charlie chortled.

"That's amazing Uncle, to think that you actually knew that kook and that he used to live right here on Perdido Isle…. It's incredible." Gaspar beamed his appreciation of not only Uncle Charlie but of his Uncle's eccentric friend George Sullivan too. "Did he make very many other crazy decrees, Uncle?"

"Oh dozens of them. Let me see, I was there when he proclaimed his most famous order, the one that received the most international attention when he told his people and the world of his decision to build a series of canals between Bolivia and both the Atlantic and Pacific Oceans. These according to the Emperor were to be built to his specifications at the expense of Bolivia's neighbors, Chile and Argentina. Now don't get me wrong Gasp, I genuinely liked this guy. Despite all his quirks and regardless of the nature of his psychological condition, Sullivan was really a visionary, and some of his *Imperial Decrees* exhibited profound foresight. He issued instructions to form a League of Nations long before anyone else ever thought of it, and he explicitly forbade any form of conflict between religions or their sects within Bolivia. I used to laugh my head off when he would become irritated at the lack of prompt obedience by the authorities to the decrees he'd issued. His everyday life was wonderfully colorful Gasp. You of all people would have approved I'm sure. Sullivan spent his days inspecting the streets of La Paz wearing an elaborate blue uniform with gold-plated epaulets, given to him by a group of officers of the Bolivian Army. Along with the dress uniform he also wore a beaver hat decorated with a peacock feather and a dark blue rosette. He frequently enhanced his regal magnificence with a gold topped cane or an elaborate umbrella dripping with tassel fringe and an ivory handle carved in the shape of a banana. As part of the inspections of his domain, Sullivan would examine the condition of the sidewalks and street cars, the state of repair of parks and other public properties in La Paz as well as the personal appearance, hygiene and proper dress of police officers he would meet on the streets. Emperor George I would also frequently give lengthy philosophical expositions on a variety of topics to anyone within earshot, while standing on a street corner."

"This is one of the best stories you've ever told me Uncle. I would love to have known Sir George." Gaspar laughed.

"I accompanied him on one of his inspections and watched him perform one of his most famous acts of 'diplomacy.' In Bolivia there were occasional anti-Chinese demonstrations in the poorer districts of La Paz. Riots, sometimes resulting in fatalities, took place. During one incident, I watched George position himself between the rioters and their Chinese targets. I was terrified for him but then he bowed his head and started reciting the Lord's Prayer in English repeatedly until the rioters dispersed without incident."

"So he was also a very brave fellow" Gaspar took note.

"Brave? Yes, you could say that." Uncle Charlie didn't sound so sure, but he was willing to give Sir George the benefit of the doubt. "Sullivan and his faithful dog Lazarus, who he insisted he'd raised from the dead, were beloved and revered not only in the Capital of La Paz but throughout the entire Bolivian Republic. Sullivan and Lazarus were known all over the country and treated as celebrities. No matter if he was dining in a private residence or at a swanky café, The Emperor always shared his meals with his mangy dog. He and Lazarus regularly ate at the finest restaurants in whatever city they were visiting and the proprietors took it upon themselves to add brass plaques near their entrances declaring 'By Appointment to his Imperial Majesty, Emperor George I of Bolivia, Protector of Alto Peru and Knight of the Holy Roman Empire.' Such 'Imperial seals of approval' were prized not only in La Paz but all over Bolivia and often insured a substantial boost in trade to those who displayed them. You would have really appreciated Old Sullivan, Gasp. For example, no play, opera, ballet or musical performance in La Paz would dare open without the management reserving an especially decorated box for The Emperor and his friends. That was my pal, George Sullivan."

Gaspar raised a disbelieving eyebrow but before he could comment, Uncle Charlie continued.

"The Emperor's reign wasn't without its pitfalls. There was an unruly policeman in La Paz named Barbier who unaware of who he was dealing with, arrested Sullivan and tried to have him committed for involuntary treatment for a mental disorder. The Emperor's arrest outraged the citizens of La Paz and sparked scathing editorials in newspapers all over South America and even here at home, especially on Perdido Isle. Capitan, Flores-Artieda, the Police Chief in La Paz ordered Sullivan released immediately and issued a formal apology to the Emperor over lunch at the Club Alemán which was given by Flores–Artieda and the entire La Paz police force in honor of Sir George. The United Press International reported that, 'The Emperor had shed no blood, robbed no person, and despoiled no country; which is more than could be said of some of the ministers in the Bolivian Government.' Sullivan magnanimously granted the errant policeman, Barbier an 'Imperial Pardon'. All of the police officers in La Paz were instructed thereafter to always salute Sullivan as he passed in the street, and some were even known to call out, 'Viva El Emperador.' The Emperor did receive some tokens of recognition regarding his exalted position from the Bolivian Government and even from some of the foreign ambassadors stationed in La Paz. The Bolivian census listed Sir George Sullivan as 50 years old and residing at Castelo del Chaco, Yungas and listed his occupation as Emperor. The Government also allowed Sullivan to issue his own money which he used to pay his bills, and it became an accepted local currency all over Bolivia. These notes came in denominations of between fifty cents and ten dollars but few were ever turned in to the Banco National for collection as they were considered collector's items even way back then. The city of La Paz also honored Sullivan by presenting him with a new Imperial regalia when his own uniform began to look a little shabby. It was a present from the mayor of La Paz who bought him a suitably regal replacement replete with gold braid, epaulets and gilded medals. In return Sullivan sent the Mayor a gracious thank you note and issued a 'patent of nobility to his excellency in perpetuity.'" Uncle Charlie finished up with a chuckle.

"Wow, Uncle Charlie, *The Emperor's New Clothes* … what you've just told me should be a movie." Gaspar enthused clapping his hands.

"But that's not the end of the story, Gasp. During the later years of Sullivans' 'Imperial Reign', he was the subject of considerable speculation. One popular story suggested he was the son of Emperor Napoleon III, and that his claim of coming from Minnesota was a ruse to hide the source of his riches. Another popular story suggested that Sullivan divorced Ida because he was planning to marry the Queen of the Netherlands. While this claim is unsupported, Sullivan did write to the Dutch Queen on several occasions, and he is reported to have met the Emperor of Brazil with whom he also discussed matters of state. Rumors also circulated that Sullivan was actually impoverished, only affecting a noble background to gain free food and perks from the public, of course we know that this was not at all the case. A number of The Emperor's decrees were duly printed in international newspapers, which Sullivan insisted were fraudulent, claiming that the newspaper editors themselves had drafted them and signed his name to them to suit their own agendas. The Municipal Museum of the City of La Paz maintains a list of the decrees believed to be genuine if you want to look into those." Uncle Charlie suggested.

"So Uncle, how does it end? What happened to his dog Lazarus, and what about his heir… his son…

Edward?" Gaspar couldn't believe what he'd been hearing.

"George died long before I did, Gaspar. I'm not exactly sure when, but you can look that up on Google if you want. I do know that he collapsed at the corner of Mercado and Ayacucho in La Paz in front of President Tejada Sorzano's town house where he had been invited to a state dinner in his honor. He collapsed just as he was about to ring the doorbell. Passersby, got the police officer on the beat who called an ambulance to convey him to Hospital. I was told by a mutual friend that Sullivan died in the arms of a cholita named Isabel before the ambulance ever arrived. Isabel was later given a pension by President Tejada Sorzano, and proclaimed the most beautiful *cholita* in La Paz.

"A cholita, you mean one of the Aymara Indian women who wear a hundred colored skirts and a bowler hat?" Gaspar had never heard the term cholita before.

"One and the same, kid." Uncle Charlie told him before taking up the story again. "The following day newspapers and wire services published George's obituary on front pages around the world under the headline 'Le Emperador est Mort' (The Emperor is Dead). I was shocked and saddened by the news but heartened by the articles. They were all written in a tone tinged with sadness, respectfully reporting that, 'on a reeking Bolivian pavement, in the darkness of a moonless night, under the dripping rain... His Imperial Highness, George

I, by the grace of God, Emperor of Bolivia, Protector of Alto Peru and Illustrious Knight of The Holy Roman Empire, entered immortality at 19:00 hours. It quickly became evident that, contrary to the rumors, Sullivan had died a multi-millionaire. Five- or six-hundred million dollars were found tucked away in a series of Swiss Bank accounts that he left to his only son, Edward. Besides his Castle in Yungas, which he had decorated with rare and valuable works of Spanish Colonial art, his lawyers discovered a vault filled with the Imperial bonds he used to sell at a fictitious 7 percent interest to tourists and fans as he walked down the streets of La Paz. They found a million dollars' worth of those worthless bonds in that vault. The old scallywag was quite a charming swindler. Ha, ha, ha…" Uncle Charlie couldn't help shaking his head and smiling with admiration.

"They also found telegrams purporting to be from the King of England, congratulating The Emperor on his forthcoming marriage to The Queen of the Netherlands, and from the President of France, predicting that such a union would be disastrous to world peace. Also found were his letters to The Queen of Spain and 10,000 shares of stock in the largest gold mine in Bolivia which turned out to be worth at least another ten million dollars to the estate. According to newspaper reports, his funeral was paid for and organized by members of the Club Alemán and the La Paz businessman's association, who provided for a handsome bronze casket and arranged for a suitably dignified Imperial farewell. Sullivans' funeral was solemn, mournful, and large. Paying their respects were members of all classes from capitalists to paupers, clergyman to pickpockets, well-dressed society ladies and those whose garb and bearing hinted of the social outcast. Some newspaper accounts reported as many as 90,000 people lined the streets of La Paz to watch the funeral cortege which stretched for two miles along the Prado to the Cathedral San Francisco. At that time the total population of La Paz was only 230,000, so the turnout was considered enormous. Sullivan was buried in the mausoleum he'd constructed for himself at the Castello in Yungas at the foot of one of the seven waterfalls on the property. The mausoleum is marked by a large stone inscribed: George I, Emperor of Bolivia, Protector of Alto Peru and Knight of the Holy Roman Empire. Later, his son Edward built a second mausoleum right next to his father's, for his mother, Ida, and had a similar stone carved which read: Her Imperial Majesty, Ida I, Empress of Bolivia, The Widow Sullivan'"

"So Uncle Charlie, what happened to his son, Edward?"

"Well as far as I know, Edward remained in South America until the outbreak of World War II, when he moved to Switzerland, probably to deliver some of his dad's money in person and in cash. Later he moved back to the States, and now and then he'd visit the house here on Perdido Isle during the season, but ultimately, he died at Locarno. He was the father of the famous Sullivan Twins. I can't wait to tell you about them."

Gaspar looked at the clock over the mantle and jumped up. "Holy Heliotrope! Uncle Charlie, we've been gabbing for hours. Al's gonna be here any minute, I promised I'd go with him to the old swimmin' hole. Let's continue this later, okay?" He yelped as he ran to the library doors, and unlocked them.

As he headed to the hall to run upstairs, throw on some trunks and grab a towel he ran smack into his Mom who was lugging a suitcase towards the front door.

"Good morning Mom." He said stopping short. "Are you going on a trip?" He asked confused. "Let me help you with that," he said grabbing the heavy bag from her hand.

"No darling, don't you remember, I'm moving to Villa Eugenia today."

"Moving? Today? I had no idea you were planning on moving out so quickly." Gaspar was surprised.

"Oh, didn't I tell you last night? I just think the sooner I start playing house over there, the better. You don't mind, do you?" she asked sweetly.

"Not at all Mom, I just didn't realize that today was the day. How can I help you?" he asked.

"Oh, I don't need any help, I'm just going to take a few things at a time, these are my overnight things, nothing important. I'll be coming and going for days, but I'm really looking forward to moving in today." She told him. "Peter's calling the phone company and the cable people. When I know the new phone number I'll let you know, but you can always reach me on my cell phone," she reminded him needlessly.

"Okay, Mom. I'm heading out to go swimming with Al and the gang. Send me a text if you need anything and I'll come right over. I can't wait to see what you do with the old place." He assured her, dragging her valise to the car and placing it inside. "Have fun Mom, I'll see you later." He gave her a kiss on the cheek before darting back into the house.

CHAPTER 8

THE BACHELOR PAD

WHEN ALEX CAME OVER TO GET HIM TO HEAD OVER TO THE OL' SWIMMIN' HOLE, GASPAR HAULED HIM into the kitchen while he fixed a couple of bacon, lettuce and tomato sandwiches that he hoped would hold them until late afternoon.

"How'd you like to move in with me, Al?" Gaspar blurted out between mouthfuls of BLT.

"Wha-da-ya mean?" Alex asked quizzically.

"My Mom's moving out, taking Lady Eugenia's house in town." Gaspar explained nonchalantly. "I'm on my own now. Thought you might like to help me turn this place into a cool bachelor pad?" He asked taking another bite of his sandwich.

"That would be great, Gasp, but to tell you the truth, I like living with my Mom and Dad. Their ideas aren't as inventive as yours or your Mom's, but I like living at home." Alex confessed. "If you ever get lonely over here, Gasp … you know you can always count on me for company. Heck, I'm just across the courtyard if you need me and I always like sleeping over whenever you ask me … but I don't think I want to move in permanently. Not right now anyway." Alex begged off.

Gaspar was surprised that given the opportunity to live independently of his parents, to do as he pleased when he pleased, that Alex would turn it down. "If it's your parents you're scared of, I can take care of them for you." Gaspar suggested, knowing that when it came to adults, he was far better at getting his way with parents than Alex would ever be.

"Naw, Gasp … that's not the problem." Alex set the story straight. I really like living next door with my Mom and Dad … honest." Alex insisted.

"I hadn't given it a lot of thought, Al. I just figured you'd like to hang out with me, and goof off all the time … you know without having to ask permission. I thought you might like to fix up the green bedroom as your personal lair? You already have your own desk across from mine in the office and the office connects with the green bedroom.

You'll have your own bathroom there too so you won't have to worry about seeing me all the time wandering around in the altogether."

"That's not the problem, Gasp. You know how much I like hanging out over here, and it would be nice, to have my own space, not that I mind your running around like a *Bawdy, Bootless, Rude-growing, Rump-fed, Swag-bellied, Knee-knocking, Rotten Banana Seller* all the time with your *Bum Bailey* hanging out." Alex Haddocked. "And I've got nothing against your lounging around in your bathtub wanting to talk all the time, but yeah, I'd rather just stay at home and come over to visit, and sleep over now and then whenever you want, but for now, let's just keep things the same as they are now, at least for the present." Alex insisted.

"You know Al, that anytime you want, you can take the other bunk in the Captain's Cabin, it's yours. I just thought it would be fun to be able to gab all night, you know, whenever the mood strikes without your having to creep back into your parents' house so you won't wake them up." Gaspar pointed out the pros and cons of his plan.

"Yeah, Gasp, I hear you." Alex enthused, "But I'm not ready to be on my own, not just yet. You know that whenever you want to invite me over for a gab session, I'm game … anytime!" he promised.

"All right then, we'll keep it status quo for now." Gaspar said, hoping he didn't sound too forlorn having his cool invitation rejected. Let's get moving, Al. Kevin and the gang aren't going to be hanging around the ol swimmin' hole all day. Come on ... we don't want to miss the fun." He urged.

When they got to the swimmin' hole, a raucous game of water polo was in full swing. Jumping off their bikes, Gaspar and Alex ran to the water's edge and without any discussion, Al dove in towards Kevin's team, and Gaspar dove in the direction of the opposite team which Flaco was heading up. No words were exchanged, it was just the way things were done down at the swimmin' hole. The game continued for three more goals before Kevin proclaimed a victory for his superior team, and everyone called it quits. Some of the kids headed home and others chose to lay out on the sand near the banks of the pond. Goofing off with their pals, had taken the better part of the afternoon. Now, Kevin, Gaspar and Alex sat side by side, soaking up the rays, talking about their latest news.

"Gaspar's asked me to move into La Rinconada with him, Kev." Alex informed his pal of the big idea.

"What's that all about?" Kevin asked

"My Mom's moved out. She prefers to live in town in a smaller house we own in Calaluna." Gaspar informed him matter of factly. It was built for my cousin Eugenia, but I don't think she ever lived there?" Gaspar told them.

"Did you have a big fight or something, man?" Kevin was stupefied.

"No, Kev. My Mom and I don't fight. It's just that she wants a simpler house, and ... you know ... she and Peter are going to be married this summer, so ... I think she just wants to set up a honeymoon house for when the time comes. It's no big deal," Gaspar assured him.

"Cool, Gasp. I think it sounds like a great idea." Kevin enthused.

"Yeah, Kev, A real bachelor pad, can you believe that Al turned me down?" Gaspar chuckled. "He prefers to live at home, keep things status quo. You know ... he only wants to come over now and then, whenever I ask him. Heck, he's there every day. I just thought it would be fun to do even more together, without having to ask permission all the time." Gaspar explained. "How about you Kev, would you like to move into the green room at La Rinconada?"

"Would I ever!" Kevin enthused, "But the possibility of it happening is slim to none, I'm afraid." Kevin shrugged. I wish I could move in with you too," Kevin dreamed, "but I'm pretty sure that my parents would never go for it."

"I didn't realize my plan was so radical." Gaspar became introspective. "I guess I'll just have to wing it alone for now guys. But if either of you ever change your mind, just pack a bag and show up."

"So what's the plan for the rest of the day?" Kevin asked, still wishing he could be a part of Gaspar's grand scheme.

"Business as usual, man." Gaspar assured him, "Just more of it." He insisted. "You're both still welcome to come over anytime … even more so than ever, Kev… and of course you guys can spend the night whenever you want … just like you've always done." Gaspar insisted. "I guess if I get too lonely for companionship, I could always get a dog." The idea just sprang into his head.

"That's a great idea," Alex jumped in.

"Yeah, Gasp, then we'd have a mascot for the club too." Kevin agreed.

"Why don't we all go back to the house right now. We can go online and look up dog breeds. We'll start with our first bachelor snack and then move on to our first bachelor dinner." Gaspar invited them. "Does that work for you, Al?"

"Let's move it." Alex shouted standing up and running for his bike.

"Anything for food." Gaspar told Kevin in an aside while rolling his eyes.

"I know, look at *That Mexican Boy* run." Kevin laughed, knowing how Alex hated it whenever one of the gang called him That Mexican Boy.

"Last one to the house is a rotten egg." Gaspar hollered, climbing onto his bike, heading for home with Kevin in hot pursuit and Alex in the lead.

When the three boys got to the house they dropped their bikes by the front steps and rushed into the entry hall.

"Let's rustle up some grub, guys." Gaspar insisted heading towards the kitchen.

Making a beeline for food, Alex and Kevin watched while Gaspar opened the refrigerator and scrounged around for something to eat. To Gaspar's embarrassment all he could come up with was some peanut butter and jelly and a few crusts of bread.

"Not a very original menu," Gaspar was less than impressed. "And there's no bacon left either. I guess we ate the last of it earlier." Gaspar told his pals sheepishly, "The cupboards pretty bare."

"So much for being the richest man in town." Kevin laughed at the meager offerings.

"Tell me about it. I had no idea that we were so under supplied." Gaspar was humiliated.

"Yikes, Gasp. If this is the best you can come up with, I think I made the right decision about the house sharing idea. Over at my place there's always tortillas y mantequila and frijoles and salsa picante." Alex bragged in Spanish. "We can go over there now if you want and get some real food, my Mom won't mind." He told them.

"These are awfully slim pickins', guys." Gaspar had to admit "Going forward this will have to be rectified." Gaspar realized. "If you like, I'll take you guys out." He offered.

"Let's go to Karen's." Alex suggested.

"Let's go to the Grand Hotel Floride." Gaspar insisted. What put that idea into his head was anyone's guess, since he much preferred the cuisine at Karen's.

"Good idea, Gasp, I could eat a horse." Alex countered.

"I can't go there in these old trunks," Kevin fretted.

"I'll lend you some pants and a shirt." Alex said.

"I'd offer you something of mine, Kev, but I know you'd never fit into any of my *midget clothes.*" Gaspar laughed. "Remember the last time I tried lending you something to wear? You looked like the giant from Gulliver's Travels in my tiny little duds." They all laughed at the recollection of Kevin trying to pull a pair of Gaspar's trousers over his hips, with the pant legs bulging as if they had been tattooed on.

"You guys go and get changed, and I'll do the same, let's meet out front in 15 minutes. We'll take the bus." Gaspar laid out the plan.

RETURN TO THE SULLIVAN MANSION

I T WAS A SHORT WAIT OUTSIDE THE GATES OF LA
RINCONADA BEFORE THE BUS ARRIVED TO WHISK THEM
over to Llojeta and the Grand Hotel Floride. On the ride
over, the three pals pulled out their phones and started
googling dog breeds.

"Would it be too corny if I got a Standard Poodle?"
Gaspar asked.

"You've gotta be kidding," Kevin laughed. "You want
a dog all clipped to look like a topiary tree?" he guffawed.

"No, I'm not talking about a dog all clipped with
pom-poms and stuff, but a big Standard Poodle is a
beautiful looking dog if it just has a puppy cut. Look

here's a picture of one." Gaspar insisted, handing his phone around.

"How about a Mexican Hairless? Alex asked earnestly.

"Are you out of your mind?" Gaspar spat looking at the picture of the pooch Alex pulled up on his phone. "It looks like a little rat, Al. I'm thinking of a big dog! Gaspar informed them.

"This one might fill the bill." Kevin enthused, passing around a picture of a Great Dane."

"It looks like a horse," Alex gave him back his phone. "You may as well get a miniature pony, Gasp." Alex laughed.

"I've always liked West Highland Terriers, and Schnauzers," Gaspar told them, "Maybe a big sized Giant Schnauzer would work." He wondered.

"Get a Labrador, Gasp," Kevin suggested. "You don't want a terrier. A big black lab would make a great housemate for you."

"Hey guys, here's our stop." Gaspar told them, putting his phone away. "We can continue this search at the counter.

Exiting the bus at the stop out in front of the hotel, the boys headed straight for the coffee shop off the lobby where they ran into Gaspar's antique dealer pal, Jason Steinmeyer sipping a cup of coffee.

"Hey Jason, mind if we join you?" Gaspar called as they approached the counter.

"Be my guest," Jason said, "What brings you chaps to Llojeta on this fine Saturday afternoon?"

"Starvation," Alex blurted out.

"We're going to have a late afternoon snack." Kevin was more specific.

"It's good to see you Jason," Gaspar smiled. "What've you been up to?"

"The usual. Antique hunting, getting my collection ready for the season so that I have wonderful, unusual offerings for my steady clients, and the tourists too, of course." He laughed.

"I've just gotten my hands on an interesting house right here in town." Gaspar filled him in. "It's full of treasure … or potential treasure … and I think it might be right up your alley." Gaspar lured the unsuspecting antique dealer into his web.

"When can I see it?" Jason asked, nearly foaming at the mouth.

"Let's go right after Al feeds his face," Gaspar suggested "I just happen to have the keys in my pocket. Hey, by the way Jason, do you like dogs?"

"I'm a dog aficionado," Jason informed his pal.

"I'm thinking of getting a dog." Gaspar filled him in on their bus ride conversation. "What do you think?"

"I think a rescue dog is the way to go. If you like, we can swing by the pound over on the mainland and see what they have to offer." Jason said helpfully.

"Okay, let's do it." Gaspar was onboard. "Al, hurry up and finish your pie!" he urged, "I mean, your second piece of pie!" he laughed. "We've got to get to the Sullivans' fast, and then to the animal shelter, rapido!" Gaspar couldn't wait.

Suitably sated with chocolate malts, French dipped sandwiches, and cherry pie, the four pals jumped into Jason's tiny convertible with Kevin scrunched into the cargo compartment behind the seats and Gaspar sat on Alex's lap.

"Go around the block, Jason. We'll enter The Sullivan Mansion from the service entrance on the next street." Gaspar directed.

"This is it, Jason." Gaspar told him as the car came to a stop outside the back gate. "We're gonna have to shimmy through the opening between the fence and the gate post until I can get these locks changed. I'm not sure Al will fit after eating two sandwiches and two malts, and two pieces of pie, but let's give it a try." He laughed.

Once on the property, Gaspar led the way to the front door, and extracting his keys unlocked all the locks. The stale air rushed towards them engulfing the four pals in its sickly-sweet odor. Slowly they crept through the dark entrance hall, all four of them once again using the flashlights on their phones for illumination. They followed the same path that Gaspar, Alex, June and Kevin had taken the day before, using caution not to trip any more booby traps. When they got to the pile of broken crystal shards from the day before, they stopped.

"Well, what do you think so far, Jason?" Gaspar asked.

"I'm speechless." Jason breathed, "What a haul. Of course there's a lot of trash, but who knows what we'll find underneath it? Look over there, you guys, that's the chassis of a Model T Ford if I'm not mistaken. What the *Drivelswiggers* would they want with a car chassis in their parlor? Jason shook his head in disbelief. "Of course all this broken Baccarat crystal is a shame. From the looks of this pile of shattered stemware, there must have been enough for 150 guests!"

"Yeah, I know," Gaspar agreed. "It was all in the rare pineapple pattern too … see." He said holding up a cut crystal fragment.

Alex didn't see what all the fuss was about and just kept his mouth shut.

Let's go back to the entrance … I want to see what's on the other side of the hall." Jason failed to hide his excited anticipation of what they might find there.

Crossing the hall, they cautiously opened the sliding mahogany doors revealing a large dining room. Like the other rooms, all four walls were piled to the ceiling with cardboard boxes and packing crates, brimming over with junk. A small corridor had been left vacant surrounding the dining room table and the dining chairs had been piled on top of the table, one on top of the other. Underneath the stacked chairs, pyramids of dishes and tea cups and serving platters and soup tureens had been pushed together in a mish mash of patterns and sizes.

"What a mess," Kevin proclaimed. "Is this supposed to be the dining room?"

Alex just shrugged, I don't know, while Gaspar shook his head yes

"No silver," was Jason's only comment as they inched their way forward, "but that Waterford chandelier is definitely 18th century, and in great condition."

"What about the table and the chairs?" Gaspar asked.

"First quality!" came Jason's breathless answer.

"DON'T OPEN THE PANTRY DOOR!" Gaspar yelled, sending Jason jumping backwards, knocking Kevin against a pile of boxes, which tumbled to the floor … but it was too late, Alex had already pulled the door leading to the butler's pantry, open. An avalanche of Coleport china came crashing down around Alex's feet as he fell backwards on his butt. Sprawled out on the oriental carpet, with his arms shielding his face, Alex squirmed backwards to get away from the splintering mountain of porcelain.

"Are you okay?" Gaspar asked, as Jason pulled Alex further away from the mess and Kevin extricated himself from the pile of fallen boxes.

"Yes … I'm okay." Alex sulked before yelling. "WHY AM I NOT SURPRISED? WHY ME? Of all the *Cockered, Clapper-Clawed, Clay Brained, Crockeried Death Tokens* … I should have known better! I'm sorry Gasp.

Now I suppose I've broken a mountain of priceless china." He fretted. "I guess you just can't take me anywhere."

"Don't berate yourself, Al." Gaspar tried to calm him down. "It's not your fault … it was an *Artless, Apple-Johned, Avalanche*." He chuckled. "As long as you're not hurt, that's all that matters." He assured his sidekick.

"What are you talking about, Gasp? That was an entire matched set of English Coleport, in the very desirable Tree of Life, pattern." Jason lamented, lovingly picking up some of the broken shards.

"You'll get over it Jason," Gaspar assured him, "There's probably lots more where that came from." He said, then wished he could take back his words wondering where the next booby trap might be. You know guys, it was impetuous of me bringing you here before we get the lights turned on, and un-booby the booby-traps. I think if Peter knew we were here now … he might not be so cool about it. Jason, would you like to take charge of cleaning this place up, throwing out the trash and arranging the good stuff so that we can get an idea of the inventory and the value?

"Nothing would please me more, give me the keys and I'll start with a crew on Monday morning. I'll check in with Peter, get the utilities turned on, and we'll start getting all these boards off the windows too." Jason assured him with enthusiasm.

"Perfect," Gaspar couldn't think of anyone better than Jason to take over the job. "Al and I will check in with you after school on Monday. I can't wait to see what you find!" Gaspar breathed a sigh of relief knowing that the Sullivan mansion and its contents were now in good and professional hands.

As they left the house, they didn't see the wizened man watching them from behind the banister at the top of the stairs with his big blackened eyes and his thin lipped, crooked smile. If they had, Gaspar would have recognized the stranger by his wrinkled old face with its pointed nose and big pointed ears. A face made more ghoulish by the thin white hairs on his pallid white head that stuck straight up in a point. The ghoul was wearing the same shirt with red and black stripes and the same round collar that he had on yesterday. When he saw Gaspar, Alex, Kevin and Jason enter the house, he didn't speak or gesture, or threaten, he just watched and waited.

• • •

Let's high-tail it to the animal shelter." Gaspar cried, squeezing onto Alex's lap in Jason's tiny sports car.

It was a short drive over the bridge that linked Perdido Isle to the mainland. The boys pulled up to the shelter with only an hour to spare before closing. Rushing into the compound they introduced themselves to the lady in charge and told her that they were looking for a dog.

With amusement at their combined energy and enthusiasm, the volunteer happily showed them around the facility, and pointed out all the dogs in the kennels. They saw Collies, and German Shepherds, mutts, and pure breeds, Maltese, Cockapoos, and Labradors in every color, as well as a big fluffy Sheep dog. Alex jumped for joy at the first Chihuahua and of course a little Mexican Hairless. Kevin couldn't believe the size of the Great Dane and urged Gaspar to get it. Jason couldn't stop looking at the Greyhound, and then discovered the big Rottweiler pacing in his cage.

"May I see the French Poodle, please." Gaspar asked the lady.

The poodle was a beautiful chocolate brown puppy, destined to grow up into a full sized Standard Poodle.

His three friends shook their heads in disbelief, but couldn't deny that the pup was a beautiful dog.

Gaspar didn't wait for discussion. "I'll take him," he told the lady impulsively. "I'll call him Mr. Peugeot."

"You're going to name your dog after a car?" Alex wrinkled his nose.

Gaspar ignored his pal, his mind was made up. "Jason, since you're the only adult here, would you take care of the paperwork while Mr. Peugeot and I get acquainted." He asked his friend, while roughing up the puppy's fur and rolling him over for a tummy rub.

"I see why you want him," Kevin agreed. "He's a beautiful little guy, Gasp. He's gonna grow up to be a very substantial and very handsome dog. Look at the size of his paws. He's gonna be bigger than you in a couple of months, Gasp." Kevin laughed.

"This is going to be fun, Al." Gaspar told his pal. "This puppy is going to be sheer luxury." He insisted. "There's nothing like a spoiled puppy to keep a guy busy." Gaspar insisted.

The boys took Mr. Peugeot out into the yard and found a ball to throw for him. The little tyke ran like the wind, and romped all over the yard, so happy to have new friends and human companionship.

It wasn't long before Jason found them and reported that all systems were go. "Mr. Peugeot is all yours, Gasp. Congratulations, you're a father now." He laughed, patting Gaspar on the back.

"Let's get going Jason. I can't wait to show Peugeot, La Rinconada. Kev, you get Al's lap, me and Peugeot will take the back." Gaspar insisted, jumping behind the bucket seats with Mr. Peugeot in hand.

While they drove back to the house, Gaspar got on his cell phone and called the Italian Grocer's in Llojeta to place an order for provisions. It didn't take long for Gaspar to place a large order with the grocer who promised to have it delivered immediately. He first asked for several bags of Solid Gold health food for puppies, and four bags of puppy treats as well as a dog collar and leash and several puppy toys, "Whatever you think a puppy would like," he told the grocer. Having taken care of

Mr. Peugeots needs, he then ordered two containers of minestrone soup, a large lasagna, a roast chicken, several containers of green beans (the only cooked vegetable he ever deigned to eat), some saffron rice, a chocolate cake and a cherry pie, and several large bottles of sparkling lemonade and apple cider. He also ordered several loaves of sliced bread, a half a pound of butter, marmalade, two packages of bacon, and a selection of cherry and apple Danish, English muffins and his favorite sugared palmetto's. He finished off with several cartons of vanilla, chocolate-mint, coffee, and double fudge chocolate ice creams, as well as a case of hot-fudge sauce, and another of caramel sauce, plus four bags of chocolate chip cookies. As an afterthought, he suggested that the grocer throw in a couple of heads of lettuce some green onions, four tomatoes, some oil and balsamic vinegar, and a couple of cloves of garlic. He secretly wondered if, he'd ever really eat any of this stuff, especially the vegetables, but told the grocer to save the order, as he might want to repeat it each week.

"That should take care of the provisions for a few days," he told his pals who'd been listening in, open mouthed as he'd placed his order.

"The four pals drove back to La Rinconada with Alex and Kevin turning around to admire the puppy and pet his head while Jason beamed at the new addition to Gaspar's family in the rear-view mirror. As they pulled into the motor court, Gaspar asked them if they'd like to stay for dinner.

"I better get home, Gasp. My Mom always likes me at home for dinner on Saturdays." Alex begged off.

"I'd love to join you." Jason accepted.

"Me too," Kevin said, "Just let me call home and tell them where I am."

When they entered the house it was as dark as a tomb.

I've got to do something about this Jason. I'm going to need a houseman to work here. Someone to turn on the lights at night, and serve the food, and do all the things my Mom used to do just yesterday." He remarked sensibly, letting Mr. Peugeot loose to explore his new digs. As Gaspar ran from room to room, turning on all the lights, the poodle pranced behind him and bounded from room to room, never leaving Gaspar's side. "Make yourselves at home guys, dinner should be delivered soon," he assured them. "There are drinks on the tray in the living room. Kev, do me a favor and fill the ice bucket from the freezer in the kitchen."

As Kevin ran to get the ice, the doorbell rang with the delivery from Llojeta.

"Come on in," Gaspar insisted, grabbing two of the heavy bags while Mr. Peugeot jumped up to welcome the delivery man who carried a big box filled to overflowing. "The kitchen's this way."

Passing Kevin in the hall, carrying a filled ice bucket, Gaspar told his pal, "Get some drinks, Kev, and bring

Jason back to the kitchen. This is going to be Peugeot's first picnic."

"I've got one more box of goodies in the truck." The delivery man told Gaspar, placing the box on the kitchen counter and giving Peugeot a pat on the head. "I'll be right back." He said as he headed back to the motor court.

"Gaspar started putting away the provisions. When he got to the lasagna, he put it in the oven and turned the dial to 350 degrees. Grabbing the Solid Gold, dog food, he poured a cereal bowl full for Peugeot and filled another bowl with water. "This is for you, Peugeot." Gaspar told the puppy lovingly, "Come and get it." He said, placing the two bowls on the floor in the corner. Having taken care of his new pal for the moment, he turned his attention back to dinner. Grabbing a head of lettuce, a bunch of green onions, and a couple of tomatoes, he decided to make a salad, and placed them in the big wooden bowl that was on the counter. Grabbing a platter from the china closet, he upturned the container of string beans onto it and pushed it to the side. The rest ended up in the refrigerator and the freezer. He was almost ready to serve a delicious repast.

The man returned with the last box, which Gaspar emptied with alacrity. Giving him a ten-dollar tip, Gaspar escorted him out the front door and thanked him for the speedy delivery.

"Come on guys," he called to Kevin and Jason, "join me in the kitchen, dinner's almost ready."

Back in the kitchen, his guests took seats at the island, and watched Gaspar make a mess out of the salad. He ripped the lettuce leaves into bits, chopped up the green onion, mashed a clove of garlic from his haul of provisions and rubbed it all over the old wooden bowl, and sliced the tomatoes up into wedges before throwing them all together in the bowl before adding olive oil and balsamic vinegar and a lot of salt and pepper. "That should do the trick." He finished out loud to nobody in particular tossing the ingredients around like a madman before setting the salad in front of his pals.

"Let's eat!" He announced, as he laid out dishes, napkins, knives and forks creating three place settings on the edge of the island. Footed glasses were filled with ice to receive the sparkling lemonade, and the lasagna was unceremoniously placed on the counter in its original tin container. Gaspar placed sterling silver serving utensils near the lasagna, the salad, and the green beans … and told his guests, "Serve yourselves, mates." Grabbing Mr. Peugeot, Gaspar sat him up on the stool next to him where the puppy watched with a big smile on his furry face as his new master entertained his pals.

Gaspar's first bachelor dinner was an enormous success. The three guys laughed their heads off telling childhood tales, and recounting local gossip while Jason regaled them with crazy tales of rich clients who were impossible, or eccentric, or both, and Gaspar petted Peugeot and scratched his ears repeatedly, bringing the puppy into the conversation. For some reason, Peugeot would bark and bark, staring across the island into thin air, but would later calm down when Gaspar told him to stop. "Why are you barking Peugeot?" Gaspar asked the pup, roughing up his tight curly fur. "There are no spirits here," he insisted, chuckling, wondering if Uncle Charlie were messing around in his own inimitable way with the new arrival.

All in all it had been a lot of fun, and Gaspar had proved that with a little help from the Italian Grocer, he could almost be self-sufficient, especially now that he had an extra mouth to feed.

Jason offered to put Kevin's bike behind the driver's seat and drive him home, an offer that Kevin accepted with alacrity. As his friends left the house, Gaspar reminded Jason one more time, "Jason, don't forget about the houseman. I'm really going to need a lot of help around here, now that I've got Peugeot too. As long as it's a bachelor pad, I think having a houseman, or valet around the house would be a good idea. I'd appreciate your help with that, okay Jason?" Gaspar asked.

"Consider it done," Jason promised, as he sat behind the wheel. Stepping on the gas, Jason and Kevin tooled down the driveway and out of sight as Gaspar and Mr. Peugeot watched from the front steps.

"Come on Peugeot. It's just you and me now." Gaspar sighed, snapping his fingers at the attentive pup, luring him back inside the entrance hall. Closing the door behind them, Gaspar proceeded to turn out the lights in all the downstairs rooms and then heading upstairs, he finally turned out the lights in the downstairs hall and the upstairs landing before leading Peugeot into The Captain's Cabin which was his fanciful bedroom. Peugeot immediately jumped up onto Gaspar's bunk and curled up like a doughnut, keeping his shining eyes fixed on his masters every move.

EDWARD SULLIVAN

D INNER HAD BEEN PLEASANT, AND GASPAR HAD REGALED JASON AND KEVIN WITH THE HISTORY OF George Sullivan just as Uncle Charlie had told him that morning. He was relieved when the others called it a day and went home. He wanted to play with Mr. Peugeot and show him around the house, and hopefully introduce him to Uncle Charlie too. Besides, he also wanted to talk some more with the old ghost about the Sullivans before going to sleep, and hoped the Charlie hadn't gone off galivanting to one of his fancy dress soirees.

The first thing he did when he got to his room was to call his mom to tell her about his day, the dinner party, and his idea of inviting Alex to share the house with him, and how Al had demurred, and the biggest news of all of course was telling her about Mr. Peugeot.

"That's nice, dear." Elvira remarked without emotion before telling him about her day, and how much she loved her new house, and that she had some decorating ideas she'd like to run by him for his opinion.

"Anytime Mom." Gaspar assured her, "I can't wait to hear what you have in mind." He told her, fearing the worst."

"Shall we meet at church tomorrow?" Elvira asked.

"I'll see you there," Gaspar promised, "Good night Mom." He rang off while grabbing Mr. Peugeot and roughing him up on the bunk, scratching behind his ears and rubbing his tummy. Suddenly, Peugeot jumped up and ran over to the desk, barking like crazy all the way.

"Uncle Charlie, are you here?" Gaspar called out. "What is it, Peugeot? Do you see spirits?" Gaspar asked the puppy lovingly.

"Present and accounted for, Gaspar." Uncle Charlie materialized, seated behind the desk, where the puppy was still barking. "What's on your mind and who have we here?" he asked, motioning to Peugeot who finally stopped barking only to turn his head back and forth in wonder at the smiling old stranger.

"Hi Uncle. This is my new pal, Mr. Peugeot. I just adopted him from the shelter. He's a rescue dog, can you believe it? What's up? Have you got a minute? Can we talk?" Gaspar asked in a rush.

"I'm all yours," Uncle Charlie, smiled, "and what a beautiful pup and a Standard Poodle too, no less. My favorite breed!" He complimented Gaspar and Peugeot. "Something tells me that I'm not going to be so invisible anymore, since apparently Mr. Peugeot can see spirits." The old ghost laughed at his latest predicament. "As you can see, I'm wearing my leisure attire so let's settle in and dish the dirt." Uncle Charlie made himself comfortable on the bunk across from Gaspar's.

"Oh, is that what you call it?" Gaspar giggled, sizing up Uncle Charlie's, Turkish fez with a tassel on it, his long dressing gown with quilted satin lapels and cuffs, and the voluminous white silk scarf tied at his neck, not to mention the embroidered carpet slippers on his feet.

"I'm dressed for staying at home tonight." so I'm all yours, and Peugeots too." The old ghost smiled at the puppy who smiled right back at him, wagging his little tail wildly. "I only wish I could pet the little tyke." He bemoaned his lack of being able to make physical contact as Peugeot jumped back up onto Gaspar's bunk and snuggled in next to his new best friend.

"Woof." Peugeot acknowledged the friendly ghost.

"Woof, right back at you." Uncle Charlie chuckled.

"He's a beauty, Gasp. A real champion. Good work boy. I always had Standard Poodles myself. A more intelligent friend will be hard to find." Uncle Charlie told him.

"You always had Standard Poodles?" Gaspar was starting to see the light. "Did you plant this idea into my head?" Gaspar asked accusingly.

"Well, yes ..." Uncle Charlie confessed. But I didn't think you'd mind. Besides, look at Peugeot, what more could you ever ask for in a loving and trusting friend." Uncle Charlie was serious.

"Thanks for the suggestion, Charlie ... I can't say that I'm not thrilled with Peugeot. He is a champion, and he's going to make a great companion now that La Rinconada is a bachelor pad again." Gaspar filled the old ghost in.

"Yeah, Gasp. Let the good times roll." Uncle Charlie chuckled. "Your mother is going to love Eugenia's house, and you and I are going to start living the life of Riley around here." He chortled with excitement. "I can't believe that your knuckle-headed pal, Alex, gave up a chance to live free of all adult supervision ... right here with you and me. What a SAP!" Uncle Charlie shook his head.

"You can't blame him, Uncle Charlie." Gaspar came to his best friends defense. "He's just a teenager, and not a very sophisticated one at that. He's lucky that he still has both parents at home to live with, and that they all like each other so much. I envy him, not that I dislike my mother, quite the contrary, but I love this house and never, ever plan to leave it. As you can imagine, Uncle, I plan to make the most of this bachelor situation, you'll see. From this moment on, life at La Rinconada is going to be nothing but fun and excitement, the dawn of a new era, to rival even your own most tinseled days of glamour." He promised the old ghost.

"That's the spirit, Gasp. Damn the torpedoes, full speed ahead!" The old boy hollered to a series of loud barks from Mr. Peugeot who was agreeing with both of his new pals in the loudest way he knew how.

"By the way, that was a jolly dinner party you gave tonight, a great way to start out your new regime," he complimented his great nephew.

"Were you there with us, Uncle?"

"I certainly was. Didn't you hear Peugeot barking at me." He chuckled. "Now tell me, what can I do for you tonight?"

"Tell me more about the Sullivans, please." Gaspar asked politely. You were going to tell me about Edward Sullivan, when I had to cut out to go swimming with Al.

"How was the water polo, did you win?" Uncle Charlie wanted to know.

"No, we lost. Kevin and Al and our pals haven't won in weeks, but today they were lucky and thrashed us."

"Too bad! What else did you do today?"

Gaspar related the rest of the day and the meeting with Jason and the visit to the old Sullivan place and the Italian Grocers, finding Peugeot, and the idea of hiring a houseman too.

"Best idea you've had in a long time, Gasp. Hiring Jason to do the dirty work is a stroke of genius and hiring a houseboy to work around here is brilliant. Make sure he's a Filipino, they're the best workers. I always had a Filipino, but maybe you'd prefer an Indian, in costume? I'll leave those details to you." He told his great, great nephew magnanimously. "Okay, let's get started with Edward Sullivan and his wife, Heddie."

"Eddie, and Heddie," Gaspar laughed, you can't make this stuff up Uncle.

"They were both beloved and maligned," Uncle Charlie told him. "Let me tell you what I remember." The old boy started. "Let's see … As much as Edward loved his father he also hated him for the way he'd treated his mother. He revered Lady Ida, and saw as much of her as possible up until her death. That's when he moved to Switzerland and rarely came back to Perdido Isle or the United States. Don't forget, all his daddy's cash was stashed in secret numbered Swiss accounts … and Edward liked to be as close to his treasure as the rest of us." Uncle Charlie winked, thinking of Gasparilla's treasure piled in the secret vault in the basement under La Rinconada. "Eddie married a Swiss girl called Heddie, and when I say Swiss, I mean German Swiss, not French Swiss, someday you'll find out that there's a difference. Remember, Gasp. If you ever get to Switzerland, it's the French Swiss that are the most fun … but I digress. Edward Sullivan wasn't the sharpest tack in the box, if you know what I mean. He managed to go through all of his father's money in about ten years, to the point of personal bankruptcy. What saved him was his bride, Heddie. She didn't come into the marriage poor, but she certainly left richer than when she started. If I told you she was stingy and penurious, I assure you I'm being extremely kind. Heddie was an eccentric miser, and was known in New York as the demon of Wall Street. She was able to accumulate more wealth than her dead father in law, the Emperor of Bolivia could ever have dreamed of. She was the daughter of a Swiss watchmaker, who along with his brother perfected the art of mass producing clocks and watches using automated production line techniques. As a six-year-old child she used to read the financial papers to her father and by 13 became the family bookkeeper. When her father died she inherited ten million dollars, which was the equivalent of a hundred million dollars today. She invested all of it in War Bonds which paid off handsomely. When her Uncle who was a bachelor left the bulk of his fortune to charity, she challenged the validity of the will in court by producing an earlier will, which allegedly left the entire estate to Heddie and included a clause invalidating any subsequent wills. Everyone who knew her wouldn't put it past Heddie to forge a new will, and against all odds, she won her case, and invested the money 'more wisely than any charity ever could,' she always bragged."

"She sounds like a real monster, Peugeot." Gaspar spoke directly to his pup looking deep into the poodle's eyes, while shaking his own head back and forth.

"Heddie was a character," Uncle Charlie insisted, "And you know how much you and I like characters, Gasp." the ghost reminded his great nephew before continuing his tale. "At the age of 33, Heddie married Edward Sullivan. Most notably for the times was the well-publicized fact that she made him renounce all rights to her money before the wedding. Prenuptial agreements of that kind were unheard of back then. The married couple moved to Edward's homes in Manhattan, Perdido Isle, and Bolivia. Shortly after the wedding, her Uncle's favorite charity tried to have her indicted for forgery based on new evidence uncovered by experts that the Uncle's will was a fake. To avoid prosecution, the newlyweds hurriedly moved to Geneva and lived in Edward's house there. Their twin boys, were born in Switzerland several years later and moved back to Chicago after the heat was off in the USA. The rumor on the street was that Heddie paid off the charity to make them go away.

"So the Sullivan twins were Swiss citizens?" Gaspar asked.

"Dual citizens, Gaspar. Their mother insisted on it … for tax purposes I suppose. She was supposed to be the richest woman in the world and also the stingiest. Heddie was not at all the motherly type. For example, when the twins would get sick, rather than summon a private doctor she would drag the kids to the local charity hospital in Chicago for treatment or when on Perdido

Isle, she'd drag them over to the mainland for the same type of free treatment. She wore only one dress, and the rumor was she never changed her underwear until it wore out, but I find that hard to believe and hope for her sake that it's not true." Uncle Charlie shuddered. "She moved back and forth between Chicago and Perdido Isle to avoid the taxman, which is something she was adroit at ... kinda like me. Because of all that, I had to admire her for her business sense if not for her dress sense." Uncle Charlie chuckled.

"She sounds like a nightmare, Uncle." Gaspar acknowledged, while roughing up Peugeot's fur. "Did you really like her?"

"Well Gasp, she wasn't warm and friendly if that's what you're asking, but she was a good egg, intelligent and that goes a long way with me. The problem was that she started to quarrel, not only with her husband but also with the domestic servants and neighborhood shopkeepers. Heddie was the largest investor in the financial house of John J. Fusco & Company. Suspecting something was up, she had the firm investigated and discovered that her husband, Edward, had not only been the firm's greatest debtor, but that management of the firm had surreptitiously used Heddie's wealth as the basis for their loans to Edward. Heddie, emphasizing that their finances were separate, withdrew her securities and deposited them with Chemical Bank, thereby causing Fusco & Company to file bankruptcy. Furious at having his debts called because of his wife's actions, Edward moved out of the house and back to Switzerland. They never saw each other again, and when he died, his ashes were sent to Bolivia in a golden urn to be placed between the caskets of his mother and father, the Empress and Emperor of Bolivia, so to speak."

"It's crazy, Uncle. What his father had done to his mother, Edward's wife also did to him." Gaspar was thunderstruck. "History certainly does repeat itself in the strangest ways."

"Well Gaspar, you have to understand, Edward was a dilettante, he considered himself a gentleman banker, but I doubt if he even knew, two plus two equals four." Uncle Charlie chuckled. "Heddie parlayed her inheritances through a lifetime of conservative investments, with substantial cash reserves to back up unexpected movement, while always keeping an exceedingly cool head amidst turmoil. With her clear-headed purpose, she was able to amass an astonishing fortune. Hers was an investment strategy to which she stuck throughout her entire life. On the other hand, her husband was a spend thrift and a dilettante. One of his more infamously extravagant purchases was a diamond-encrusted chamber pot. After Eddie and Heddie divorced, he became an ardent philatelist and assembled one of the finest private stamp collections in the world. Edward ultimately married a gal called Nelly, who had been his long-time 'housekeeper.' A woman who Heddie insisted was a former housemaid of hers that Edward had met in Geneva. Edward's friends, spurred on by Heddie, wholeheartedly disapproved of Nelly, and dropped poor Edward like a hot potato. Despite reports that Edward had spent or lost most of his father's vast fortune, Heddie insisted that the $1 million yearly return on the remaining $100 million dollars from his inheritance was adequate to Edwards most expensive needs and that she had no intention of augmenting it with her own hard-earned money. She told anyone who would listen, including the press that 'Throwing good money after bad was not part of her investment strategy.' The newspapers estimated that at the time of Edward's death he left Nelly one hundred thousand dollars, along with ten million dollars in unpaid debts. Nothing of Edward's passed on to his twin sons, except the house on Perdido Isle, and the house in Chicago, which had been given to Heddie outright in the divorce."

"This is sure a complicated family, Uncle Charlie," Gaspar yawned.

"I understand, Gasp. But let me just tell you a few more amusing details so that you can better understand Heddie's special quirks." Uncle Charlie insisted. "For example, she never turned on the heat in her houses nor used hot water, not even to bathe. She did not wash her hands as often as you and I do, and she rode around town in an old Model T Ford, although she owned three Rolls Royce Phaetons. She ate mostly pies that cost fifteen cents each and expected her family and guests to eat the same. One tale claims that she spent half a night searching her house for a lost two cent stamp. She even instructed her laundress to wash only the dirtiest parts of her dresses, like the hems or the cuffs, to save money on soap. Someone told me that she ate only oatmeal, heated on a radiator, which I had to laugh at since I knew from firsthand experience that she never turned on the heat, and only ate fifteen cent pies. In her old age she developed a bad hernia, but refused to have an operation because it cost $150. She suffered many strokes and ultimately had to rely on a wheelchair. Heddie was 81 when she died right here on Perdido Isle. Apparently, she died of apoplexy over an argument with her maid about the virtues of skimmed milk. That debate was the straw that broke the camel's back and caused the strokes that finally did her in. Estimates of her net worth ranged from $1.9 to $3.8 billion, making her arguably the richest woman in the world at the time. She was buried in Switzerland, next to her mother and father, having converted late in life to their Episcopalian faith so that they could be interred together.

"Did she ever do any good with her money?" Gaspar wanted to know, "Did she ever perform an act of random kindness." He was getting bored and so was Mr. Peugeot too, hearing about the stingy old lady.

"Good question, Gasp. There's no doubt that she was a successful businesswoman who dealt mainly in real estate and railroads, and she was also known to lend money. For example, the City of Chicago came to Heddie in need of loans to keep the city afloat on several occasions. On one of these, she wrote a check for $1.1 million and took her payment in short-term revenue bonds. She was always insistent on being paid back with interest of course and she was known to travel thousands of miles to collect a debt that was due, even if it were just for a few hundred dollars. To answer your question, no. The woman was a nightmare." Uncle Charlie put the nail in Heddie's coffin.

"What about the twins, Uncle ... tell me a little about the twins." Gaspar could barely keep his eyes open and Mr. Peugeot had already given up and was snoring softly having retired to the foot of Gaspar's bunk.

"The twins lived with Heddie until her death. She disapproved of all of her children's friends suspecting that they only liked them because of her money. Although she had several magnificent homes to choose from, Heddie and the twins moved repeatedly among small apartments in Chicago, and Hoboken, New Jersey, mainly to avoid establishing a residence permanent enough to attract the attention of tax officials in any state. Because they were here, on Perdido Isle when she died, the twins settled in, and for all practical purposes never left." Uncle Charlie chuckled, as Gaspar closed his eyes and fell fast asleep.

CHAPTER 10

A RUDE AWAKENING

GASPAR OPENED HIS EYES AND SAT UP WITH A START. HE WAS SURPRISED TO FIND THAT HE WAS FULLY dressed, and still on top of the covers. Mr. Peugeot was still snoozing, curled up snug against him. He suddenly realized that he'd fallen asleep last night right in the middle of Uncle Charlie's narrative.

What a *Loggerheaded, Dizzy Eyed, Dismal Dreaming Diplodocus*, he thought. "You fell asleep right in the middle of the good part." He berated himself out loud causing Mr. Peugeot to jump up, and stare deep into his master's eyes while tipping his curly head left and right. Peugeot was so funny he made Gaspar laugh. His response was to grab his puppy's ears and pet the poodle's wet nose.

"You can say that again." Uncle Charlie said from the bunk opposite, causing Peugeot to bark like crazy in his direction. "Did you have a good night's sleep?" The ghost asked solicitously waving his hands at Peugeot, hoping the hound would shut-up.

"Well, yes …" Gaspar gave his answer some thought, grabbing Peugeot by the collar and pulling him down onto his lap, "but I must say, I had some wild dreams, that all took place inside the Sullivan mansion, and there was that weird guy—the ghoul. He was here and there and everywhere in my dream, just watching me all the time and Peugeot of course who was guarding me just like the good dog he is." Gaspar petted the affectionate pooch, while rubbing his own nose against Peugeots cold wet snout.

"That's interesting, Gasp. Can you describe him?"

"Peugeot?"

"NO, the ghoul." Uncle Charlie wondered how much longer he was going to have to play second fiddle to a French poodle.

"Well, he's old, and thin, with dark circles around his eyes, and a wide, thin lipped smile on his old wrinkled face. Unlike Mr. Peugeot here, he hasn't got a lot of hair on his head, just a few strands standing straight up and he has big pixie-like pointed ears. Just like yours Peugeot, but not as handsome." He told his puppy. "Oh … and he's wearing a red and black horizontally striped shirt with a round collar." Gaspar always prided himself on taking inventory of people and places that he saw, even in his dreams. "He's the dude I saw up in the window of the carriage house the first day we saw the old Sullivan place." He finished up his description and rolled Peugeot over on his back lovingly rubbing the dog's belly.

"Sounds like a very unattractive character." Uncle Charlie shuddered, looking askance at Gaspar's vigorous massage of Peugeot's tummy.

Gaspar looked at the clock and jumped up, "Yikes, Uncle Charlie! I've gotta get up and get dressed. Come on Peugeot, it's almost time for church, I promised your grandma I'd be there." He told the pup confidentially. "After church Uncle Charlie, me and Al and Peugeot have to hightail it over to the Villa Gaspar, it's club day you know." He shouted over his shoulder, while running into the bathroom, pulling off his wrinkled clothes from yesterday followed by the happily barking Peugeot of the wagging tail.

Uncle Charlie watched as the half-naked teenager and his chocolate brown standard poodle, raced each other into the bathroom, and just shook his head. Well, now I know who's top dog in this house, and it ain't me anymore, he thought to himself, sadly shaking his head before disappearing through the wall.

After a quick shower, which Peugeot was happy to supervise from his perch on a fluffy bath mat, Gaspar threw on his Sunday best, and ran downstairs with Mr. Peugeot now on an elegant red leather leash. He was just in time to join Alex and Felix and Angela as they headed out the door to go to church. It was a Sunday tradition, church followed by breakfast at Karen's Café, after which, Gaspar and Alex would spend the day with their buddies at the Villa Gaspar in Llojeta that Gaspar had turned into a club for his classmates.

"You're not bringing that French hound to church, are you?" Alex feigned surprise.

"I certainly am. Peugeot is a Catholic and if he hasn't been baptized, I'll make sure he will be shortly." Gaspar insisted.

"What's his name?" Angela asked sweetly, hunkering down to get eye to eye with the new addition to La Rinconada.

"His name is Mr. Peugeot." Gaspar told her.

"That is going to be a very big dog, Gaspar." Felix warned him.

"I know, Felix. Isn't he a wonderful boy?" Gaspar enthused, leading the pooch to the waiting car.

"Wha be da dawg?" La Mar asked in his distinctive patois.

"This is my new pal, La Mar. His name is Mr. Peugeot." Gaspar introduced them.

"He be one big Frensch dawg someday," La Mar intoned. "Do he bite?"

"He hasn't yet, La Mar, but there's always a first time." Gaspar warned him. "Come on Peugeot, jump in the back of the woody. It's time to go to church."

Seated in a big booth at Karen's, Peter piped up and asked Gaspar and Alex "Besides adopting this really great pup, what have you guys been up to?" Mr. Peugeot was seated up on the banquette between Peter and Gaspar. Between the two of them it was hard to tell who liked Peugeot better.

"Well, I've been doing some research on the Sullivans," Gaspar fibbed but it was only a little white lie, considering all of his information came from Uncle Charlie. "And yesterday we went swimming down at the ol swimming hole with Kevin and the gang. When we were done we were so hungry Alex Kevin and I ended up at The Grand Hotel Floride coffee shop. We ran into Jason there." Gaspar filled them in. "I was so pleased to see Jason, I told him all about the Sullivan place and then we all went over to show him the mansion."

"The Sullivan mansion?" Peter arched his eyebrows, "You went back to the Sullivan mansion with Alex, Kevin and Jason?

Too much information, Gaspar thought, swallowing hard. "Yeah, Peter, I decided that running into Jason was fortuitous. Of all the people we know, Jason is the best man for the job of cleaning out the junk from that place, and making sense out of what's worth keeping and what's worth throwing away." Gaspar made himself clear. "I've hired Jason to do the job, Peter. You two can hash out the business part of it between yourselves tomorrow."

"You didn't go inside the house, did you?" concern rose in Peter's voice.

"Of course we did, Peter," Gaspar thought it best to nip any concern in the bud. "And if you can imagine … Al triggered another booby trap, and we lost a small fortune in antique English Coleport china in the famous Tree of Life pattern! But like I told Jason, there's probably more where that came from, and by that I meant porcelain as well as booby traps!" Gaspar made light of the danger to life and limb the booby-trapped mansion offered. "Anyway, the best part of the day was finding Peugeot at the animal rescue, and bringing him home." He hugged Peugeot and gave him a treat from a bit of left over pancake saturated with maple syrup.

Peter pretended not to be impressed by the visit to the mansion, and chuckled at the puppy gobbling bits of pancake from Gaspar's dish.

Looking around the table at the faces of his family and friends, each registering a different emotion, Gaspar piped up. "I know it's probably not good for him, but I find Peugeot, irresistible." That seemed to put any question of who might come first in Gaspar's affections to rest.

"What did you learn about the Sullivans, Gasp?" Elvira dreamily changed the subject.

"I'll have to tell you another time, Mom. It's time Peugeot, Al and I head over to the club house." Gaspar extricated himself as best he could, wolfing down the last bite of his pancakes that Peugeot had selflessly left for him. "Let's go!" he told Al as Peugeot dragged him out the door to the waiting woody.

"Wait for me," Al called, running behind him with a slice of buttered toast between his teeth."

• • •

Mr. Peugeot, was a big hit with the kids at the club house. Except for the poodle's presence it was a typical day at Villa Gaspar, with swimming, games, lunch and a lot of horsing around, but as the day wore on, Gaspar became less and less engaged in what the others were doing and realized that as much as he liked hanging out with Peugeot and his pals, he was pre-occupied with the Sullivan saga and wanted to get back to business. It didn't take him long to come to a decision. He had to find Alex and take action. Finally with Peugeot on the end of a leash he found Al in his favorite place, the soda fountain, slurping up a chocolate soda.

"Al, hold down the fort." Gaspar begged his friend. "I've got an errand to run, Peugeot wants to go out … but we'll be back in time for dinner." Gaspar promised.

"What're you up to, Gasp? Don't you want me to go with you?"

"Not this time, Al. I've got something on my mind, and I've got Peugeot to watch out for me. Stay here and play host in my absence. Besides, Peugeot and I will be right back."

Without further discussion, Gaspar snuck out the side door and grabbed one of the bikes from the garage. It was only a few minutes ride to the Sullivan mansion, and his heart was pounding in his throat the entire trip as Peugeot trotted alongside, keeping pace with the bike. Reaching his goal he left the bike against the fence and shimmied onto the property, helping Peugeot up onto the wall where he easily followed his master through the chink in the fence. As they passed the carriage house he looked up at the second-floor window, horrified at the prospect of what he might see there, but the window was empty. They worked their way through the garden, and up the front steps to the wide door in silence. Taking out his keys, he let Peugeot inside and held a finger to his lips hoping the pooch would understand his need for silence. Again the stale air rushed out of the house as they crossed the threshold side by side. He purposely left the door wide open to let in what little late afternoon sunlight the covered porch offered. This time he didn't go left or right but lead Peugeot straight ahead. The long central hall had many doors leading off of it, all of which he was too scared to open. He knew where the living room, dining room, and withdrawing rooms were. He ascertained from yesterday's visit where the butler's pantry was, and with an innate sense of architecture settled on a large pair of sliding doors to open, knowing instinctively that behind them was the Sullivans' library.

"Follow me, Peugeot." He whispered to his stalwart canine companion.

He opened the doors cautiously, and used the flashlight on his phone to illuminate what he could of the darkened space. Taking a deep breath, he walked into the room and stood under the elaborate chandelier. Shining his light in a 360-degree arc, he took note of the walls of tall bookcases fully stacked with leather bound volumes. Over the fireplace was the family portrait by John Singer Sargent that Uncle Charlie had told him about, and there was a comfortable Chesterfield sofa, and several English club chairs arranged for conversation. There was also a large Chippendale desk, at one end of the room, and up against every wall were hundreds of boxes, stacked two and three deep, and three and five boxes tall, each box spilling over with detritus. There were also similar boxes stacked behind the sofa and on three sides of the magnificent mahogany desk. More boxes filled to overflowing were stacked in the corners of the Chesterfield sofa, and on the seats of the club chairs too. Behind the desk a monumental doorway led into what Gaspar could only guess would be a game room, billiard room, or maybe an English pub-like bar. Before he could stop himself, he pulled the doors open, and before he could jump back he heard, more than felt, the avalanche of wooden shelves and leather-bound books which plummeted down on top of him. What he didn't hear was the sudden high-pitched bark that emanated from Mr. Peugeot, or the wail of the little dog as his master hit the ground.

• • •

"When Gaspar came to, he had no idea where he was or how he'd gotten there. He was in a dark room, and his body ached all over. There was something heavy covering his legs and body, and there was the sound of dull heavy thuds all around him. When he turned his head, his vision was obstructed by large jagged objects to his left and right and also by Peugeot. The little dog was standing over him, licking his face then darting away, whimpering and barking, obviously frustrated at not being better able to help his master. Unable to move, he started to panic as the dull thuds became louder and more urgent. Slowly his legs seemed to become unpinned, lighter, and easier to move. Similarly his abdomen was released, and next his arms as Peugeot continued darting back and forth, whimpering and barking between licking his face and panting over him with hot frantic breaths. When the sharp pointed objects disappeared from each side of his head, he was able to see left and right again, but suddenly he wished he couldn't. Looking straight up the only thing he could see in the dim light was the face of horror. Looking straight down at him were two dark ringed eyes set into the cruelest of wrinkled faces. Course white hairs stood up straight from his almost bald pate, and a wide paralyzed grin framed by thin black lips dared Gaspar not to scream. The ghoul's ears were large and pointed framing his face and accentuating his pointed chin and cone like hair. This was the devil incarnate, and Gaspar was his prisoner. His only solace was the reappearance of Peugeot who continued his frantic whimpering, barking and face licking while darting in and out of sight.

Finally finding his voice, Gaspar screamed, "Be gone, *You Bald-Headed Budgerigar!* Unhand me and let me and my dog leave this place, you *Loathsome Body Snatcher.* My friends will be looking for me soon, and they know that I'm here, so be warned you *Miserable Molecule of Mildew*, Mr. Peugeot and I will have no truck with any *Brutish Highwayman attempting to hold us prisoners.*" He Captain Haddocked to the best of his ability under the circumstances.

"Be calm young Sahib," came the words of the monster in a sweet, sing-song voice. "I am not *hoing to garm you...* Going to harm you." he corrected himself. "I am only here to *yelp hou* young sir. He garbled his words again. You were engulfed in books by one of my master's many booby traps. I helped him set them up and now I'm sorry that you have *pallen frey* to one." The creature apologized in his peculiarly garbled speech.

"*Pallen frey?*" you mean Fallen Prey? Right?" Gaspar was amused but confused and in a little bit of pain.

Gaspar still lay on the ground motionless as the stranger tossed more books off to the side, while Peugeot, sat still as he continued to cover Gaspar's face with wet kisses. Ultimately the ghoul managed to free Gaspar's four-foot-eleven, ninety-pound frame. Very gently the man removed Gaspar's sneakers and placing his skeletal hand on Gaspar's forehead as he asked, "Are you able to *tiggle your woes*, Maharaja?"

"*Tiggle my Woes*, Gaspar giggled, then wiggled his toes, and nodded yes. Peugeot wanting to help began licking Gaspar's bare toes, which caused Gaspar to giggle and wriggle, "Peugeot, stop that right now." Gaspar insisted.

"Very well, Sir. Let me know if there is any sharp pain." His ghoulish rescuer asked as he squeezed Gaspar's legs and then his arms. "No sharp pains, Sahib?"

Gaspar shook his head no, reaching over and pulling Peugeot over to him protectively.

"Very well Maharaja, I will *yelp hou* up now." With that the old man, cradled Gaspar's neck and helped him up into a sitting position. Gaspar released Peugeot who sat back and barked his approval as the stranger grabbed Gaspar under his armpits, lifting the teenager to a standing position.

Gaspar was light headed and started falling backwards but the man held him up and guided him slowly out through the library door and down the hall to the staircase, with Peugeot close on his heels. "*Hit sere* Saab."

He instructed, easing him down so he could sit on the bottom step. "I will bring you *wome sater.*" He promised.

As he scurried back down the hall, Peugeot jumped up onto the step and sat close to Gaspar, who put his arm around his loyal companion.

"Bring me *wome sater*?" Gaspar repeated the garbled words to Peugeot who listened to his every word intently. Giving the garbled words some thought, he finally realized that the man had just offered to bring him some water. "That's a curious speech impediment, I must say," he told Peugeot while lovingly scratching the dogs ears.

Less than a minute passed when the stranger reappeared carrying a cut crystal glass of water. "Drink this young prince. You will *beel fetter.*"

"I certainly hope I '*beel fetter*' or feel better," Gaspar told Peugeot, before taking a gulp of the clear liquid. He immediately choked on the poison, and spat it out! Whatever it was, it certainly wasn't water! "WHAT'S THIS!" he coughed and sputtered, "What are you trying to do … poison me?" he yelled hoarsely pushing the glass back into the monster's hand as Peugeot barked furiously at Gaspar's assailant.

"A *pillion mardons*, Maharaja, please don't, munish pe. It is all we have to drink here, there is no pater in the wipes, the bottle label does not say poison, young master, it says *Gombay Bin.*"

"A Million Pardons, Water in the Pipes, Bombay Gin!" One gulp of the gin, and Gaspar's head was completely cleared. "What goes on here? Who are you and why are you living in this house?"

"I am Rajeev, master. I am the *haretaker of this couse*. Mr. and Mr. Sullivan are my employers. You are welcome here too."

"Rajeev, you're the Sullivan brothers' Indian servant? I've heard of you!" Gaspar remembered Karen's dismissive mention of the foreign towelhead. "Where's your turban, Rajeev?" Gaspar blurted out, instinctively and then not waiting for an answer withdrew the question and replaced it with another. "How is it that you've been living here alone all these years? The Sullivan brothers died ten years ago. How have you survived, how do you live?" Gaspar was confused and Peugeot registered his confusion too with a sideways tip of his head.

"I live above the carriage house, Sahib. There is a tunnel that connects the carriage house with this house and another that connects the two guest houses as well. My provisions are delivered every week from the Italian Grocers in Llojeta. Their bill is paid by my employers lawyers in Chicago. It is only a week now that the *wights and later* ... lights and water," he corrected himself, "and gas have been turned off. And my weekly delivery of provisions also seems to have ceased. At least the grocers failed to appear on schedule last week, and the mailman hasn't delivered my bank statement showing that my pay has been deposited into my account in Chicago. I fear that after all these years of soyal lervice that I have been completely abandoned by my employers, Sir." Rajeev told his sad plight to Gaspar and Peugeot, his voice trembling with fear and trepidation.

Peugeot showed his sympathy with a sharp, high-pitched whistling whine.

"Don't be scared Rajeev, don't fret, everything will be all right. Your masters' lawyers have given up this house. They are no longer going to be responsible for it, and I'm afraid that means you too. I am the owner of the house now. From now on you can work for me if you like, or if you'd rather return to India, I can help you with that too. Starting tomorrow my workmen are going to start cleaning this place up. It would be good if you could work with them and show them where the booby traps are. show them the ropes, so to speak. Would you like to do that Rajeev, would you like to work for me from now on?" Gaspar petted Peugeot instinctively.

"Oh yes, Maharaja. Rajeev would like that very much. Your *cish is my wommand*, young Prince." Rajeev said, bowing low, then corrected himself, "wish is my command."

"By the way, Rajeev, this is my friend, Peugeot. He and I are inseparable." Gaspar smiled, pulling Peugeot closer to him.

Before Rajeev could respond with as much as a how de do, a great pounding of shoe leather, on the front porch caught their attention. Peugeot let out a furious series of barks as Peter Cawthorne, Jason Steinmeyer, Alex Mendoza and two policemen from the Llojeta station rushed up the front steps, crossed the porch, and burst into the very dark house. Focusing flashlights on Gaspar seated on the step next to Peugeot who kept up his barking and Rajeev looking ghoulish, as well as startled and afraid, the police drew their weapons and ordered Rajeev to freeze.

"Gaspar, are you okay? Has this fiend harmed you in any way?" Peter asked rushing up to his young friend, client and future stepson.

"Not at all, Peter." Gaspar stood up with an out-stretched hand motioning the officers to back off and unhand Rajeev. "This is my friend, Rajeev. He just saved my life." Gaspar informed them. "It's a long story, Peter, and it will all make sense to you in good time." He assured the assembled posse.

"Gasp, what happened to you?" Alex asked anxiously. "It's eleven o'clock at night. When you didn't show up at the clubhouse for dinner and the movie, I started to get worried. I called Peter and he called the cops. We've been looking everywhere for you, but when we found your bike out back, we knew we'd find you here." he explained, reaching down and giving Peugeot a pat on the head.

"I can't explain my urge to explore this place all by myself, but thank God, Rajeev was here or you'd-a probably found me dead under a pile of books and garbage." Gaspar smiled wanly. "Do me a favor guys," Gaspar addressed the police. "Please take my pal, Rajeev to the Grand Hotel Floride. Tell the manager that he is my guest and that anything he wants, he gets. And while you're there gents, please go to the coffee shop and have a late-night dinner on me … I insist." Then to Rajeev he spoke calmly. "Rajeev, go with my friends, order room service, and pajamas and a tooth brush, anything you want, and when you're rested have the hotel car bring you back here tomorrow. This is my friend Jason Steinmeyer. He's in charge of cleaning this place up. Please show him and his crew everything … especially where the booby traps are!" Gaspar chuckled, ruffing up Peugeot's fur. "I know Jason will appreciate that information more than anything else … don't you think, Peugeot?" he addressed the dog, while looking at Jason who was standing off to the side of the entrance hall, staying out of the way but shaking his head in agreement to what Gaspar was saying.

"Okay Peter, Okay Al, let's get back to La Rinconada. This has been a longer day than I ever bargained for." He laughed, shaking the policeman's hands and patting Jason on the back before taking Rajeev by the hand and walking him and Peugeot out of the house to the waiting patrol car. When Peugeot jumped into the back seat, Gaspar laughed. "Come on Peugeot, stop playing around, you're coming with me."

CHAPTER 11

MONDAY-MONDAY

THE NEXT MORNING, EVERY BONE IN GASPAR'S BODY ACHED. NOW HE KNEW WHAT IT FELT LIKE TO BE beaten to a pulp. Barely able to walk to the bathroom he checked himself out in the mirror and couldn't believe what he saw reflected there. HIS FIRST BLACK EYE! He couldn't have been more proud, but Gaspar decided there and then that 'there was no way in Hades' he was going to school today no matter how much he wanted to show off his shiner.

He immediately called Alex and told him of his aching bones and his decision to skip school, while Mr. Peugeot, sitting by his side, tried to figure out what all the fuss was about.

"You lucky dog, are you sure you don't want me to hang around?" Alex hoped.

"… it's not necessary, Al. I don't need a male nurse yet." Gaspar joked. Come visit me in the Captain's cabin before you head out… and Al, bring me a raw steak from the frig… will ya? Wait till you see my shiner, man … it's a beaut!" He insisted before signing off.

Next, he called his mom over at her house and told her about his accident and how miserable he was feeling this morning.

"That's nice dear," was her only response.

Gaspar loved his mom because she was so detached, and let him do whatever he wanted within reason and never asked any questions. "Do you need me to do anything or bring you anything dear?" she asked solicitously, but Gaspar knew better than to ask her to follow through.

"No Mom, Alex is bringing a raw steak to put on my eye. I'll be fine." He assured her before saying, "goodbye."

"Come on Peugeot. We need a hot bath." He told his pooch.

He then returned to the bathroom, with Peugeot prancing behind him, to turn on the taps and fill the tub. When the tub was filled and steaming hot, he threw in a couple of handfuls of Epsom salts and slid under the bubbles. Peugeot stood up on his hind legs with his front paws on the rim of the tub to make sure his master really knew what he was doing.

This should do the trick, Peugeot," Gaspar assured the concerned puppy, as he relaxed under the hot water just as Alex bounded through the door without knocking.

"Hey Gasp, here's your steak. I sure wish I wasn't going to school today."

"I feel like a ton of bricks fell on top of me..." Gaspar moaned, "It may have been a ton of books and wooden shelves, but believe me Al, my bones are aching like it was a ton of bricks."

"You lucky dog, by the way, great black eye, dude." Alex marveled, placing the dish of raw steak onto the lip of the marble tub where Peugeot sniffed it in hopes it was for him. "Do ya think you'll recover anytime soon?" Alex asked, obviously jealous of his friends magnificent shiner and his ability to ditch class.

"Probably the minute the school bell rings this morning, Al." Gaspar chuckled as he squirmed under the hot water. "Listen, Al. Have La Mar drive you to school then tell him to come back here in case I start to feel better."

"You think you'll be well enough to get to school a little later?"

"Nah, but I might feel well enough to go to the old Sullivan place and see what Jason has uncovered." Gaspar chuckled mischievously. "You better get going, Al ... you don't want to be late. I'll send La Mar to pick you up after school if you want to come by the Sullivan place and see our progress." He giggled, holding up the raw steak for Peugeot to sniff again and give a couple of licks to, before slapping it onto his tender black eye. "And Al, invite Kevin and June to come with you after school too." He insisted. "Do me a favor, pal. On your way out, ask your mother to make me some chicken broth and buttered toast. I'll call downstairs when I'm out of the tub and ready to eat it ... okay?" The invalid feigned complete helplessness.

"Gaspar, if I didn't like you so much ... I think I'd hate you." Alex told his best friend in no uncertain terms. Of all the *Blue Blistering Bell-Bottomed Balderdash*, you're what Captain Haddock would have called, a *Tin-Hatted, Black-Eyed Tyrant*, or even worse, a *Twisted Black-Eyed Turncoat!* Or maybe even... a *Two-Timing Black-Eyed Troglodyte!* And just for the record, as far as being my best pal is concerned, if you can't get me out of going to school today too, then your nothing but a *Black-Eyed, Bathtub Admiral* and that's saying a lot!" Alex finished off, laughing hysterically at his latest off the cuff Haddock curses as he closed the bathroom door behind him.

"AND STAY OUT..." Gaspar yelled after his best friend, laughing hysterically. "What a riot your Uncle Alex is, don't you think Peugeot?" he asked the confused dog who tipped his head and let out a stream of high pitched barks not knowing if his two friends were fighting or playing around. Then he turned quickly and started barking furiously in the direction of the sink.

"Well you two are certainly having a lot of fun this morning." Uncle Charlie noted from his perch on top of the sink directly across from the bathtub. "I was there last night, joined the search party and heard everything." He told his great nephew. "That was a close call, Gasp. What crawled over your liver to make you go to the old Sullivan place alone without even telling Alex, let alone me, that you were going there? Uncle Charlie was dead serious, waving at Peugeot in hopes of stopping the pups incessant barking.

"It was that dream I had, Uncle. The face in the window, something told me that I had to go over there and explore. That was definitely a bad idea, but all's well that ends well. At least I solved the mystery of the ghoul in the window … it was just the Sullivans' sweet old Indian servant, Rajeev. I'll have to call the hotel later and see how the old boy's doing." Gaspar made a mental note.

"Do you think he'll be able to tell you all you want to know about the Sullivan Twins." Uncle Charlie asked facetiously. "Or would you like me to continue where I left off, before you hightailed it to church yesterday morning." He asked, raising an eyebrow at Peugeot who starred at him with his head tipped sideways, mesmerized by the ghostly presence.

"I'm sorry I ran out on you, Uncle Charlie. Please finish what you were telling me… I'm all ears." Gaspar implored.

"Well let's see, just before you suddenly found religion, I had just finished telling you about the death of the Sullivan twins mother, Heddie, and how they decided to stay put on Perdido Isle. But that's not the whole story. One of the twins was called Tommy and the other was Timmy. Tommy styled himself a musician, and nicknamed himself 'Moon Kitty'. Timmy was no less a dilettante. He was a self-styled woman hater, who went by the moniker, Brother Man. They were both nutty as fruitcakes. They weren't always hermits or recluses. After their mother died, they actually made an attempt to live somewhat normal lives but it was obvious that they were a little bit buggy, if you know what I mean. Whenever Tommy was approached on the street by a woman he would always shuffle away with downcast eyes, not ever wanting to make eye contact with a female. It must have been a reaction caused by his uncaring mother." Uncle Charlie speculated. "As for Timmy, his problem was quite the opposite. He was always seeking female companionship as much as possible until one of the objects of his affection didn't return his love in the way that he wanted her to. That's when he turned inwards just like his brother. I think it was at that time that both brothers decided to hole up in their house and avoid all females completely. On the other hand, they were considered generous hosts whenever a male passerby or an old school chum visited them. Food and drink at the Sullivan mansion was always plentiful. Whenever they were invited out as a reciprocal invitation, the brothers always refused saying that their business affairs, at home, required their full-time attention. I'd say sometime after

1980, I doubt if either brother ever left the house, except at night when they went scavenging for junk in Perdido Isle's trashcans and back alleys.

Before he became so reclusive, Moon Kitty, or Tommy liked to hang out on his front porch playing the bongos. Bongo drums were his instrument of choice which he made himself using buffalo skin. He told anyone who asked that he designed his own clothes based on the robes of the Norse God, Odin. Because of his quirky get ups, he was nicknamed by the locals as *The Viking of Perdido Isle*. Although he wasn't blind, Tommy taught himself Braille, and subsequently music, from books written in Braille, which he sent away for by mail order. Before they went completely reclusive the brothers entertained such notable musicians as Leonard Bernstein, Arturo Toscanini and legendary jazz performers and composers, Charlie Parker and James Morrison, too. I used to attend some of those crazy jam sessions." Uncle Charlie reminisced.

"Uncle Charlie, you amaze me. Such colorful characters and so sad, too." Gaspar shook his head, while Peugeot still sat motionless on the bathroom floor, mesmerized by Uncle Charlie's presence.

"Yeah, you would have loved Moon Kitty, Gasp… especially when he performed the bongos at home wearing his horned Viking helmet." Uncle Charlie laughed. I'll never forget the night he imported an entire tribe of Blackfoot Indians to perform their traditional native Sun Dance. He brought them in from Idaho, and accompanied them on the bongos. That was a night to remember on Perdido Isle, for sure." Uncle Charlie guffawed. "If you can believe it he even sued a little-known disc jockey for stealing his name, calling his radio show, 'Moon Kitty's Symphony Hour' and believe it or not, he won a million-dollar settlement and thanked James Morrison and Arturo Toscanini in the newspapers for testifying in his favor."

"What a scream, Uncle. You can't make this stuff up." Gaspar enthused, isn't that right Peugeot?" he asked the dog who wagged his tail furiously in answer before returning his full attention to staring at Uncle Charlie.

"Oh that's not all Gasp. I attended several musicals in that house, and let me tell you something ... they were sheer hell. Moon Kitty's idea of music was based on street sounds like what you'd here in a subway or from a foghorn, something that real musicians would call 'snake time'. He was always telling me, 'I'm not planning on dieting in four-quarter-time.'" Uncle Charlie couldn't stop laughing at his memories of Moon Kitty. "Believe it or not, Moon Kitty was actually invited by Philip Glass to conduct the Brooklyn Philharmonic Chamber Orchestra at the New Music America Festival in Brooklyn. Glass thought Moon Kitty's work on bongos might help stimulate young people to adopt a renewed interest in classical music. I think the invitation scared Tommy out of his wits, and sealed his fate as far as becoming a full-fledged recluse in his own house. At least I don't remember seeing him out on the streets after reading that announcement in the press." Uncle Charlie recounted. Back in the 1950s he actually did release several recordings on 78s and lps of his bongo music, but I only know this because he sent them to everyone on Perdido Isle as a gift. A couple of weeks later he followed up the gifts by sending everyone who got one a bill, which I can assure you none of us paid! Either way, I guess nobody in their right minds would have bothered to buy them … that's for sure.

"And Timmy or Brother Man, what about him, Uncle?"

"Brother Man was a horse of a different color. When he was a kid he lost the sight in one eye when his mother, Heddie, refused to take him to a doctor after he fell down the stairs. The result was the loss of his eye which Heddie refused to replace with a glass one so Brother Man had to wear an eye patch up until the day she died. After the funeral the first thing he did was to go to Dr. Stevens, in downtown Llojeta and order a dozen glass eyes. His favorite one had the union jack displayed right in the middle of it. He was forever taking it out and cleaning it and then putting it back in and asking whoever was at hand, friend, or stranger on the street, if it was in straight or if the flag was sideways or upside down. During the summers when it gets so hot and humid on the Gulf, he would cut the arms off of his jackets which he wore with shorts and old tennis shoes.

If you ever get into his closets you're gonna find some interesting items besides his brother's Viking gear." Uncle Charlie chortled. "Timmy once told me that he owned 365 handkerchiefs, one for every day of the year and the same number in dress shirts. Despite all his wealth, he always traveled third class and carried his own valise in order to avoid having to tip a porter. That was before he and his brother shut themselves off from the world of course." Uncle Charlie made himself clear. "Brother Man, went through a lot of sartorial phases, the last one I remember was his lederhosen craze. For a long time he only wore lederhosen and expected everyone on Perdido Isle to follow suit ... which of course none of us did." Uncle Charlie chuckled. "The last time I saw Brother Man out and about, he was walking a lobster on a leash right out in front of the Grand Hotel Floride. When I asked what he was up to he told me, 'I'm exercising my lunch.' That's one of my last memory of seeing him out on the streets.

"A lobster on a leash ... lunch ... you've gotta be kidding." Gaspar guffawed. "You'd like to chase that lobster I bet, Peugeot?" he asked the dog who was now sprawled on the blue marble floor near the bathtub, bored by the conversation.

"Not at all, he also had a pet hedgehog and a jackdaw that he'd trained to follow him around without a leash." Uncle Charlie insisted. Thanks to Timmy Sullivan, Perdido Isle was graced for a long time with an extraordinary assemblage of blue, yellow, and pink doves, which Brother Man had dyed and let loose to decorate the neighborhood. It was a beautiful sight, but unfortunately these have all died off or flown the coop." Uncle Charlie lamented. "Brother Mann was into animal husbandry. He told me that at their ranch in Texas he had a bull named Jupiter that he'd trained to act like a horse so that he could ride it all over the range and use it to pull his carriage. He also told me that he'd ridden Jupiter in a fox hunt in Virginia, using pigs as pointers instead of dogs and that he'd tried to train an otter to fish but getting the otter to let go of his catch proved impossible. Timmy showed up at the Grand Hotel Floride one day in a lambskin hat with a brim nine-feet in diameter and a waistcoat made entirely of duck feathers. That was one of the best get-ups I ever saw! At parties at the Sullivan mansion, Brother Man would blow his hunting horn to announce that dinner was served. I'll never forget the night that the repast was served from his brother's favorite coffin. That was quite a night. Brother Man was wore a toga and insisted that all dinner conversation would be conducted in sign language.

"The silence must have been deafening." Gaspar couldn't believe Charlie's story.

"If you think that's eccentric," Uncle Charlie continued, "when his mother, Heddie died, Brother Man advertised for twelve old maids to follow the coffin from the church to the cemetery to the tune of a fiddler and a bagpiper who were selected to accompany his brother who walked with them while playing on bongo. They were instructed to play only happy songs, nothing somber or dirge like. According to the newspaper reports only two old maids showed up and the priest wouldn't let the musicians play anything but O'er the hills and far away, after forbidding Moon Kitty from playing the bongo's at all. When they read Moon Kitty's will, after the tragedy, it was published that he'd left the head of the IRS a piece of rope to 'go hang himself with'. We all thought it was a touching bequest. When we buried Brother Man after the tragedy he had left instructions to use the coffin that he'd had specially built with windows and shelves inside. He used to keep that particular coffin in the front room of the mansion and charged people to sit in it the years before he became such a shut in."

"Hold everything Uncle," Gaspar begged, removing the steak from his eye and handing it to Peugeot who had instantly sprung to attention. "This is for you, baby." He told the delighted dog, who ran to the corner of the bathroom and started tearing the steak apart. Stepping out of the now tepid tub, Gaspar announced, "I've gotta dry off, Uncle... let's continue this story in the next room." He suggested wrapping himself in a towel and heading back into the Captain's Cabin.

Wrapped in a terry cloth robe and curled up in bed, Gaspar picked up the phone and imitating a very fragile invalid, he asked Angela in the kitchen if she could bring up "the chicken broth and buttered toast."

"May I continue, Gaspar?" Uncle Charlie asked from the other end of the bunk where he'd perched, down by his nephew's feet. I haven't got all day you know. I've got a date for lunch with a señorita at the Alhambra and I'd like to finish this tale before that hound comes back and forces me to give up my perch on the end of what he thinks is HIS BED!" The old ghost winked while keeping a dramatic but pretend, scowl on his face.

"Carry on, Uncle, I know you love Peugeot as much as I do. Gaspar insisted. You're just mad that he barks every time you're near so you can't sneak up on me anymore, or spy on me in secret either." Gaspar laughed, hitting the nail on the head. Okay, continue please, I'm all ears, at least until Angela knocks with my breakfast tray.

"As I was saying… The Twins, were a little bit like you and me. They were compulsive collectors. Unlike us, they not only liked to buy expensive antiques and works of art, but they also went in for discarded newspapers, books, outdated medical equipment, pianos and their mother's old Model T Ford. The utilities thing is nothing new, Gasp. The brothers had been living without gas, electricity, water, or telephone service for nearly a decade before the tragedy that killed them. Booby-trapped tunnels traversed the ceiling-high piles of junk. Police officers, responding to an anonymous call, found Timmy's body in one of these cubby holes made out of boxes, his clothes in tatters, his knees doubled under his chin where they had been frozen into position by arthritis years before. Surrounding him were more than 150 tons of junk and rusting treasures. It took police and removal crews several more days to find Tommy's body, although it lay only feet away from Timmy's, hidden by stacks of newspapers bound together with twine that had buried him alive when he accidentally triggered one of his own booby-traps. You see, Timmy was a cripple and relied on Tommy to take care of him. When Tommy died in one of his own collapsing piles of debris, Timmy just starved to death in his miserable cubby hole.

"But what about Rajeev? Why didn't he come to their rescue?" Gaspar wondered.

"When the cops questioned the Hindu servant, he told them that he only entered the house once a week to bring in the food which was delivered regularly from the Italian Grocer in Llojeta." Uncle Charlie laid out the facts. "When he brought in the food one day and saw that all the food from the week before was untouched. He was worried for his masters but couldn't get through the maze of trash to find out if they were dead or alive. "Rajeev is the one who called the police. He told them that he finally went inside to look for his employers, but it wasn't until he found his way blocked by an avalanche of old newspapers that he decided to call the cops. The cops later told me all the grotesque details of the story, what they found, the stench of decay that permeated the place, the desperate squalor. When I think of the former, charmingly eccentric Sullivan Twins, isolated and now certifiably insane, living inside that dark, shuttered, unlighted mansion, it breaks my heart." Uncle Charlie choked up.

"I wonder if they ever thought about the real world that they had known or if they were both living some fantasy existence in their solitude?" Gaspar asked Charlie, not expecting an answer.

"They weren't really alone," Uncle Charlie threw in, " Tommy and Timmy received lots of information about life in the outside world from the detritus and objects that they found in back alleys and brought into the house. Bundles of newspapers were like information deposited into the house, by the wind. You see, Gasp, Tommy and Timmy, before they became incapacitated, were night crawlers. They scoured the alleys and back streets of Perdido Isle after midnight picking up trash. Don't be surprised at what you find inside that house. The cops who found the bodies, told me about piles of World War II gas masks, army boots, and old army fatigues, stacks of newspapers tied with string and boxes and boxes of old vinyl records, probably Moon Kitty's old recordings, who knows? Timmy was always talking about amassing an extensive newspaper archive that would demonstrate the cyclical nature of history. His plan was to cut and paste what he found into one single mega-newspaper in which each major category or event—war, crime, murder, automobile accidents, etc. would be rendered in its archetypal, timeless form. One single huge newspaper that would cover all the news for the rest of time with no need for updating or reprinting, ever. He explained to me that 'for a nickel, the reader would have a portrait in newsprint of life on earth,' complete with the news 'of his own impending death, which would be dutifully recorded as a number in the blank box on the last page under the heading Obituaries.'" Uncle Charlie shook his head sadly.

"Well I've seen a lot of the newspapers piled up in that old house, Uncle, but something tells me the twins never got around to cutting and pasting them." Gaspar murmured. "I kind of feel sad that they never accomplished their goal with that timeless newspaper."

"Don't feel sorry for the Sullivan Twins, Gasp. By our very natures as Americans, we are a nation that celebrates individuality, independence, and extravagant consumption as one of our national values. If you think about it, Tommy and Timmy were, by virtue of their very eccentricities, paradoxically American icons of individuality and freedom."

"I like the way you think, Uncle." Gaspar complimented the old ghost. "You better get moving if you're going to make your lunch appointment in Spain. Angela should be here any minute with my soup and toast and then, if I feel better, I think I'll head out to the Sullivan place and see what Jason's up to." Gaspar grinned, knowing that he hadn't pulled any wool over Uncle Charlie's eyes and that the old ghost knew full well that his mischievous great nephew never had any intention of staying in bed all day.

"Have a blast, Gasp." Uncle Charlie called as he stood up from the end of the bunk, "You deserve a day off, you really should stay in bed you know…. even though I know your not going to." He called as he disappeared through the floor, to Mr. Peugeots consternation

CHAPTER 12

WHAT JASON FOUND

IT WAS TWO O'CLOCK BY THE TIME GASPAR ARRIVED AT THE OLD HOUSE. JASON HAD BEEN BUSY ALL MORNING, throwing out trash. A huge forty-foot container stood in the motor court off of the service entrance and a gang of Jason's hired *braceros* were going back and forth from the house dumping piles of *scrap* into it. When Gaspar entered the house, what he saw was mind-bogglingly marvelous. Jason had a gang of carpenters working all morning, pulling the old wooden planks off the windows, and now sunlight streamed into the house filtered only by the filth still left on the window glass and the cloud of dust particles swirling through the still fetid air.

"What a difference, Peugeot." Gaspar marveled as Jason stepped forward to welcome him and his hound.

"Gasp, I'm glad you're here." Jason welcomed his friend while squatting down to welcome Mr. Peugeot too. I didn't think I'd see you two today after what you both went through last night. By the way, that's a great shiner, buddy." He complimented Gaspar on his terrifically effective black eye.

"Thank you very much, Jason, that's what I thought too. "It's my first shiner, by the way." He announced proudly. Wild horses couldn't have kept me and Peugeot away from here, this afternoon. What have you found for me … anything exciting … any treasure?"

"Come with me," Jason insisted. Just look at this place." He marched Gaspar and Peugeot upstairs where every corridor was still piled high with walls of boxes and every doorway was blocked with a fallen down mess. "It seems between you and Alex that you've managed to find most of the booby traps downstairs. This morning, Rajeev helped me find all of the booby traps up here. We'll have to excavate this mess in the hall before we can get into any of these rooms. By the way, that's where they found Tommy he said pointing to a spot between two walls of bound stacks of newspapers and over there is where Timmy starved to death," he said pointing to a little cave-like alcove made out of old boxes and more bound newspapers. "Just thought you'd like to know." Jason told his ever-inquisitive pal with a shudder while Peugeot stood in front of the Alcove, barking bloody murder.

While Peugeot barked his heart out, Gaspar said a silent prayer for the unlucky twins before following Jason downstairs with Peugeot hot on his heels.

"Look in here, Gasp. We've cleared most of the living room, come in and check it out."

Gaspar stood in the doorway of the living room and looked around. With all the boxes of trash gone, what he now saw was a beautifully proportioned room, elegantly paneled in antique 18th century, French boiserie paneling painted with a cream-colored ground, and carved details picked out in gold. To Gaspar's delight, each panel held beautifully framed French paintings, stacked one above the other to the ceiling.

"Check out the carpet, Gasp. It's Savonnerie, 18th century. Look at it carefully, it's in quite good condition considering what's been going on here for the past few decades… it's worth a couple of hundred thousand in New York if you want to sell it. Once its cleaned, it might actually be attractive." Jason pointed out its qualities, while Peugeot sniffed around looking for a good place where he could Christen it.

"Come on Peugeot, don't get any crazy ideas about peeing on my new carpet." Gaspar laughed. Having been busted, Peugeot pranced over to where Jason was now rhapsodizing over the curtains and how wonderful they were. The old silk damask draperies hung in tatters at the windows so torn that Gaspar could see sunlight shining through them, but Gaspar had to admit they were beautiful in their decrepit state.

"You may as well throw those out Jason." Gaspar's suggestion was quickly seconded by Mr. Peugeot who immediately lifted his leg against one of the rotten old silk draperies.

"I agree, Gasp, but knowing how you like seeing things the way they used to be, at least once, I didn't want to deprive you of the pleasure of seeing this marvelous, rotting old silk up close and personal, Jason chuckled.

"Thank you very much, Jason. We understand each other perfectly and Peugeot has also given them his mark of approval too!" Gaspar laughed at his naughty puppy who was looking very guilty and terribly sorry that he'd let loose on his master's rotted antique silk damask. "What did you find in all those boxes that used to be in here? Gaspar asked.

"If there was anything even slightly valuable in here, I've had it sent out to the carriage house." Jason told him. "Wait till you see that marvelous old stable, Gasp … it's fantastic." Jason whetted Gaspar's appetite. "Let's see, besides all the trash we threw out this morning, which consists mostly of old newspapers, I've saved a great collection of old magazines for you. I've sent them all to the carriage house. I'm sure you won't want to keep all of them, but there's a lot of old *Country Life*, and *Realities* and *Connoisseur* magazines that might interest you." Jason told him. If you decide that you don't want them, I'll be happy to take them off your hands. Just let me know." The antique dealer told him.

"If I don't want them, they're yours Jason." Gaspar assured his friend.

"We also found a mountain of old gas masks, which we can probably sell to the swap meet market along with dozens of army boots, and army fatigues and boxes and boxes of old lp records with bongo music on them."

Gaspar had to laugh but urged Jason to continue. "What about me? Is there anything else for me?" Gaspar asked knowing that Jason knew exactly what he meant.

"So far, the best stuff I've found is just what you see in front of you. That's a good bronze Dore and baccarat crystal chandelier." Jason told him, pointing to the massive light fixture hanging from the ceiling. "And the boiserie's are 18th century. In fact, I can probably tell you exactly which chateau they came from just as soon as I can find a minute to do some research." Jason promised. All the furniture is good … a mix of 18th and 19th century French furniture, not museum worthy, but very decorative and worth a chunk of money if you want to sell any of it. The paintings are Barbizon school, old Sullivan must have paid a fortune for them, but the market for Barbizon paintings isn't as strong today as it was in the 1920s, however, all 16 of them would probably bring a couple of million at auction unless you want to keep them for yourself of course?" Jason queried.

"Not my favorite kind of art." Gaspar mumbled, looking over the pastoral scenes depicting sheep's and cows grazing in green fields with blue skies and fluffy clouds. "On the other hand, the Singer Sergeant hanging over the fireplace in the library interests me … a lot." Gaspar confessed.

"It's a great painting," Jason agreed wholeheartedly, as Mr. Peugeot barked his approval.

"Have you ordered new window glass yet for where ever it's needed, Jason? And how about the structure? Is it sound, found any dry rot or noticed any termite infestation? Do you think we need to replace all the windows?" Gaspar rattled off the laundry list he'd been taking mental note of since the first day he'd seen the house.

"Mike Fitzpatrick's on the job, and I've asked him all those questions. He's around here someplace. When we run into him we'll get the latest information available." Jason promised.

Mr. Peugeot's loud barking announced the presence of an intruder, as a distinguished old oriental prince entered the room. The elegant visitor was dressed in fine pink silks embroidered with gold threads studded with stones and on his head was a large pink turban with a long trailing tail running down the potentate's back. An intricately set jewel sparkled above his forehead where it had been pinned to the elaborate turban. It took Gaspar a moment to figure out who the intruder was and then he realized it was Rajeev!

"Rajeev, what a change! Is this what you usually wear around the house?" Gaspar greeted the old servant.

"This is what I used to wear around the house, when I came to work for Mr. Sullivan and Mr. Sullivan. I was *bust a joy* then, it was *yany mears* ago. Now that I am working for you, Sahib, I want to make a good impression."

"You certainly have done that, Rajeev." Gaspar couldn't help giggling at the servant's garbled speech and theatrical get-up. "What do you think so far, Rajeev. The old place is starting to shape up, little by little. Is it starting to look like the way you remember it from the good old days?" Gaspar asked.

"It looks very fine, Maharaja." Rajeev, bowed. "Just like I remember it." The servant beamed. "Please tell me how I *san cerve* you today, master." He insisted.

"Oh, just carry on Rajeev, and help Mr. Steinmeyer here in any way you can … I'm sure he'll find lots of ways to keep you busy…" Gaspar passed the buck.

"I live to serve you master." Rajeev, bowed again, and backed out of the room while Peugeot growled to himself, seemingly suspicious of all that pink silk. "I'll await your command in the entrance hall Sir." Rajeev addressed Jason.

"He's all yours, Jason." Gaspar chuckled when Rajeev was out of earshot. "Do your thing, Maharaja." He giggled to Jason under his breath. "Now Maharaja,"

Gaspar joked to Jason, "show me some more rooms. Surely you've excavated more than just this one parlor."

"Oh yes, there's more, *Sahib*." Jason joked back, "Follow me boys," he said, whistling at Peugeot to follow them.

The three friends entered the second parlor, where Alex was almost clobbered by a mountain of cut crystal goblets only a few days ago. The mess had been cleaned up and the wooden boards had been removed from the windows. The second parlor was almost a carbon copy of the first with a matching chandelier and walls paneled in the same cream and gold painted carved French boiserie's. Most of the boxes had been cleared from around the walls, but in this room every surface was now covered with clocks. Some of them were the most elaborate in every size and shape that Gaspar had ever seen.

"Where did all these clocks come from, Jason? I've never seen so many in one room."

"They were all shoved one on top of the other in all those boxes that were piled up everywhere. It's an amazing collection ... and look, not just clocks ... watches, pocket watches, lapel watches, wrist watches, watches stuck into alligator wallets, watches set into little church towers in paintings, pocket watches, men's watches, ladies jeweled watches on jeweled chains, even stop-watches, and none of them working ... not one." Jason sighed.

"The room where time stood still." Gaspar joked. "Only clocks and watches, nothing else?" Gaspar was slightly disappointed as he picked up one of the time pieces and wound the key on its back then placing it back down without any hope that it might actually start ticking. "What about the library? Besides the painting by Sargent, are there any books that interest you?" he asked, placing the clock back where he found it and walking back out into the hall. Peugeot, stood motionless starring at the clock tipping his head back and forth to the gentle tick tock suddenly emanating from the jeweled timepiece.

"Follow me, *Maharaja*, I always save the best for last." Jason assured him, whistling again, for Mr. Peugeot to fall in line.

The dark and foreboding library where Gaspar nearly lost his life only 24 hours ago was now filled with light which highlighted a cloud of floating dust particles that never seemed to land on any solid surface. Gaspar was dumbstruck by the sight of all those floor to ceiling mahogany bookcases … stuffed to bursting with Moroccan leather bindings stamped in gold.

"My kind of room." Gaspar exclaimed, standing near the center table, spinning around to take in all four walls. "The chandeliers a beauty, Jason. Do you think they're Tiffany?" *Gaspar took a guess as to the maker*, amused to see Peugeot mimic his every move, spinning around to see the entire room too.

"You're right-on, Gasp. Good call." Jason complimented his friend's connoisseurship. "But look at the books, all first editions no doubt. It's going to take a long time to catalog all of this. Maybe you should send Margaret down to help us in here?" Jason suggested referring to Margaret Stewart, Gaspar's personal librarian at La Rinconada.

"Good idea, I'll get her over here tomorrow." Gaspar promised. "The family portrait by Sargent is worth the entire house, don't you think?" Gaspar asked his friend, forming a personal connection with the artist by shortening his name like he might for an old friend or family member. "That's Sir George and Lady Ida, and their only son Edward." Gaspar informed his antiquarian friend. "He's the father of the Sullivan Twins." Gaspar filled Jason in on the family genealogy portrayed in the painting. "It's beautiful, don't you think? Look at the date, Jason, 1925. It's supposed to be the last painting Sargent ever painted." Gaspar wanted to let the expert know that he'd done his homework, thanks to Uncle Charlie, who Gaspar considered his ultra-secret weapon!

"Wow, Gasp. You really have done your homework, Jason complimented him. Do you want to know what's behind the door you opened before you were clobbered by that mountain of falling books last night?" Jason asked, walking over to the double doors.

"Be careful Jason." "Those doors are lethal!" Gaspar yelled, jumping forward to stop his friend while Peugeot barked a loud warning of his own!

"Calm down, Gasp. You used up the booby trap last night. We've already been in here this morning. Look,"

He said, pulling the doors open before Gaspar or Peugeot could stop him, "it's a vault. I've already called Morey, the locksmith in Calaluna to get over here to open for us. He promised to come over this afternoon, so stick around if you want to watch."

"Of course I will, thanks for telling me. I know Al will want to be here too, he's probably never been to a safe-cracking party before, Jason." There was nothing Gaspar loved more than an impromptu party.

"Did I hear someone call my name," Alex asked striding into the room followed by Kevin and June and Morrie from Emerson's Locks in Calaluna as Mr. Peugeot bounded towards them in greeting. "Wow, Gasp. What a difference a day makes." Al marveled, grabbing Peugeot by the ears and scratching his head lovingly.

"Twenty-four little hours," Gaspar sang. "My favorite song."

"Huh?" Alex didn't get it.

"It's a song, Al. 'What A Difference A Day Makes', I'll explain it to you later." June offered graciously, bending down to rub her nose against Mr. Peugeot's.

"Hey, Gasp. Great Shiner." Kevin gave his pal the thumbs up.

"Oh my, June exclaimed. Does it hurt?" Her look of concern broke Gaspar's heart.

"It's not as bad as it looks, June." Gaspar assured her. "Can you believe what Jason has uncovered around here already? Look at all this great stuff." Gaspar remarked changing the subject.

"Hi, Gaspar, big house." Morrie piped up, not in the least bit impressed with his surroundings.

"Hi Morrie. Come on in … this is Mr. Peugeot," He introduced the dog, "and what you're looking for is right here." Gaspar motioned to the huge armored doors of the built-in vault. "I hope you don't mind if we watch you work you're magic?"

"Not at all," Morrie answered, "Take a seat kids, this may take a while." He told his young audience, mysteriously.

"Cool Gasp, this is better than when that old Mexican newscaster opened Al Capone's vault on TV, way back when I was just a kid." Alex thought back to a long forgotten safe cracking fiasco filmed for television.

Everyone sat down and watched anxiously, holding their breaths, as Morrie stepped to the safe. The locksmith studied the dials carefully. With great care he took out his handkerchief and wiped the dials. Slowly he turned each dial, listening carefully to the clicking of the workings with his ear pressed up against the armored doors. Then suddenly, without any fanfare, and very little effort, Morrie twirled the big dial and opened the safe, reset it and locked it up again. "That should do the trick." Morrie stood up nonchalantly. Taking a small pad of paper from his pocket and a pen, he made a notation on the top sheet and ripped it from the pad with a flourish. Handing the scribble to Gaspar he said, "Here's the new combination, I'll send you my bill in the morning." Without another word, Morrie left the room and continued to his next appointment.

"Wait a minute Morrie." Gaspar called after the safe locksmith.

"Yes?" Morrie turned around in the doorway. "Have you another lock for me to fix?"

"Well no … I just wanted to say that … err … that wasn't much of a show Morrie," Gaspar complained.

"A show?" Morrie pretended not to understand.

"I just hope you're not planning to charge me a lot for this job, Morrie" Gaspar joked. "Considering you had a captive audience, I would have expected you to add a little more mystery to your performance." Gaspar teased the workman. "Before you go, at least tell us it was the hardest safe cracking job you've ever had to do." Gaspar begged, but Morrie was already turning on his heals preparing to leave the room.

"You have the new combination for the safe, Mr. Brown." He told his customer dully over his shoulder.

"Thank you very much, Morrie." Gaspar said, folding the paper and putting it in his pocket.

"Glad to be of service Mr. Brown" Morrie turned around to face his audience before disappearing through the door. "I'll send the bill to Mr. Cawthorne, as usual." Morrie took his leave with as little enthusiasm and excitement as he had shown when he'd arrived. "Hope you find what you're looking for in the vault." He mumbled. "Big house," he looked around the interior again disinterestedly, "I used to trick or treat here when I was your age. Always wondered what was inside. Looks like a lot of old junk to me." he added as he backed out of the room, suitably unimpressed. "Better put some steak on that eye." He mumbled his word to the wise and then without warning he took off his cap and made a deep theatrical bow to his delighted and astounded young audience as they simultaneously broke into loud applause for his virtuoso performance, Peugeot barking his approval to the cries of "Encore, encore" coming from the collective lungs of Gaspar and his pals.

After Morrie was out the door, Gaspar looked at Jason, Kevin, June, Alex and Peugeot, who tipped his head at him questioningly before they all started laughing hysterically. "Well that was a non-event, Kevin drawled, before they all turned their attention back to the vault.

"Aren't you going to open it, Gasp?" Alex asked.

"If you guys don't mind, I'd rather save that pleasure for later. Right now, I'd like Jason to show us what he's been up to here. The safe can wait." Gaspar had no idea what might be inside but if it was at all valuable, he wanted to keep that information close to his vest.

"Follow me Lady and Gentlemen and pooch," Jason suggested, "Let me show you some of the progress I've made around here."

As Jason showed the gang around the house, they couldn't believe what they were seeing.

"Check it out, Al." Gaspar insisted, wha-da-ya think?"

"Incredible. I can't believe all the old stuff in here, what-cha gonna do with it, Gasp… throw it out?

Gaspar gave his best friend a withering look and Peugeot growled his master's annoyance.

"Oh yeah, I forgot, you like all this old used stuff, umm…Aah…*antiques*." Alex pulled himself out of the ditch he'd just dug for himself.

"Gaspar, a lot of this stuff is beautiful," June enthused, "Look at these gorgeous urns… imagine them filled with flowering fruit tree branches." She suggested.

"They're French, June." Jason informed her, "Second Empire."

"I've never seen anything like them." She enthused.

"If you like them, June, you can have them." Gaspar offered the treasure to his friend, "Don't forget to take them with you when you leave." He insisted, as Peugeot sat wagging his tail furiously while smiling up at June.

"You've got to be kidding." Kevin butted in. "June, you can't take valuable presents from strange men." Her brother insisted. "What would mom and dad say?" he chuckled.

"If Gaspar wants to give June a present, let him do it." Alex couldn't understand what the fuss was all about. "What's the big deal, they're just old junk. They don't even have any nicks or cracks on them."

Peugeot growled again, letting Gaspar know that he knew Alex was a Philistine.

"Let's check out the carriage house, Gasp." Jason diplomatically changed the subject, successfully leading the teenagers out of the house.

Gaspar was pleased to leave the debate over the French urns behind him, and looked forward to his first peek at the interior of the carriage house. Standing between the two massive doors which Jason had opened wide, Gaspar couldn't believe the beauty of the old stables. The interior of the carriage house was entirely decorated with intricately detailed white painted paneling picked out with bright red highlights. Down the center of the cavernous space Jason had started piling the boxes of junk which held possible treasure not destined for the dumpster.

"Check this out, Gasp… *GAS MASKS*! Wow, *AND BOOTS TOO*, Army Boots, Gasp! Oh groovy, look, old records, we still have an old record player at home, maybe my mom and dad would like some of these. Hey cool, *BONGO MUSIC*, by some dude named Moon Kitty! This stuff is really groovy man." Alex enthused over the contents of the many boxes.

Gaspar wasn't surprised by Al's reaction to the boxes of flea market junk. Privately, he despaired at the possibility of ever educating his best pal about the difference between trash and treasure. All he could do after Alex's last remark was to shake his head at Jason, who rolled his eyes in silent agreement along with Peugeot who tipped his head with a mournful look in his watery eyes.

"Hey Gasp, look at the towelhead, Alex laughed, as Rajeev entered the carriage house.

"The man in the turban is Rajeev, *You Blister Brained Tadpole*. You met him last night." Gaspar reminded his slightly slow sidekick.

"Oh, hi Rajeev, sorry I didn't recognize you in your fancy dress … and ah, oh yeah, sorry I called your, a, what-ja-ma-jigger, a towel-head or whatever." Alex hung his head in embarrassment and went back to picking through more old boxes of junk.

"May I *yerve sou* and *gour yuests* some refreshments, Sahib?" Rajeev asked, garbling his words in a double Spoonerism. "Serve you and your guests," he corrected himself without the slightest embarrassment.

"That would be nice, Rajeev," Gaspar giggled, but what have you got to offer? I don't want any more of that fire water you served me last night." Gaspar insisted.

"*NO, NO, MAHARAJA!*" Rajeev was mortified, "I will *sever nerve* you, I mean *never serve* you anything from Bombay, ever again." He promised his master. "I have fresh fruit juice from the Italian Grocers," he offered, "let me bring *sou yome*?" he garbled his words yet again.

"Very well, Rajeev." Gaspar had to giggle, "Carry on." Gaspar commanded with a flick of his wrist. "*I could get used to this kind of service in a hurry,*" he told Kevin as an aside, "but it's not easy trying to figure out what he's saying all the time." He giggled again and Kevin and June joined in.

Jason showed them more boxes, some filled with sheet music, and some filled with old crystal goblets. There were boxes of mismatched dishes, and boxes filled with old baseball cards. Barrels held athletic equipment including baseball bats, catchers mitts, golf clubs, golf balls, tennis rackets, and tennis balls, and there were also crates and crates of mismatched playing cards.

"Some of these catchers mitts are pretty cool, Gasp." Kevin commented. "Look at this one, it's an old Rawlings model, and look … it actually has Mickey Mantle's signature on it!"

"You can have it, Kev. Take any of this stuff you want," Gaspar insisted.

"One of those sold to a movie star back in the 90s for $250,000.00 Gasp. Are you sure you want to just give it away?" Jason was always the big businessman looking out for his clients and ultimately his own best interests.

"It's yours Kev if you want it." Gaspar's decision was final.

"Check this out, June" Jason offered, changing tack. "Look at all these old handbags." He suggested walking over to a mountain of boxes some of which were open.

Inside were hundreds of ladies hand bags, some in leather, some in silk, some in alligator and some in lizard. They were every size and shape some with elaborate clasps and some without. There were bags that were in beautiful condition and others that were ready to be thrown out.

"Why are you keeping some of these, Jason? Look at this one, it's ready for the trash." Gaspar insisted.

"I learned a long time ago when I was working my first garage sale, never sell or throw-out a purse or a wallet until you've checked its insides thoroughly." Jason instructed his young friends. "Someday, we'll have time to go through all of these but until then, they'll stay right here. I know because I once found a real diamond brooch pinned to a bag, and another time I found one with a genuine diamond ring inside. I've also found a lot of left-over money too. I once picked up five hundred dollars by just going through the purses at a sale. People forget to look inside before they put things up for sale and that can be a big mistake!" Jason told them. "The same is true of birthday cards and Christmas cards." He informed them, "I collected a thousand dollars once just going through old cards before tossing them away."

"What's all that stuff under that tarp over there?" Gaspar asked pointing to a mountain of stuff under a dirty stained tarp.

"Pianos! So far, we've found 14 piano's or the equivalent of 14 piano's in various states of disrepair. Some are just carcasses and some are just the insides. The twins had concert grand pianos, baby grand pianos, several upright pianos and at least three-square pianos. I think if nothing else we can salvage the ivory off of the keys. but who knows?" Jason shrugged they may all be salvageable.

"Where's the Model T?" Gaspar asked.

"It's over there, Gasp. I've started another pile of garbage just for scrap metal, and as you can see, it's getting pretty high." Jason chuckled. "I'm not sure you know this, Gasp, but the twins were using the engine of that Model T to generate electricity. It's surprising that they didn't die of carbon monoxide poisoning or burn the house down with all the gasoline they were using to run that contraption inside the house."

"Holy Moly," Kevin couldn't believe his eyes when Gaspar uncovered the twins home- made electrical generator made out of an old Model T.

"Gasp, Kev, June … get over here quick and check this out." Alex shouted frantically from across the room, as Peugeot bounded protectively towards the sound of Al's agitated voice. "Look you guys… COMIC BOOKS, hundreds of them." He waved a handful up in the air with excitement, to Peugeot's growling dismay.

"Groovy Al," Gaspar drawled unimpressed, as Kevin ran behind Peugeot to see what all the fuss was about. "Those comic books should keep them busy while we go back into the house and look at the really good stuff." He whispered to Jason and June in an aside.

WHAT GASPAR AND PEUGEOT FOUND

LATELY, GASPAR'S LIFE HAD BEEN IN QUITE A BIT OF TURMOIL. JASON HAD SUCCESSFULLY FOUND HIM A GREAT Filipino houseman named Angelito, who was turning out to be essential to his life at La Rinconada. Angelito was a dream come true. While Angela cooked and ran the house, Angelito was there to serve and do Gaspar's bidding, day and night. If he came home late after Angela had left for the day, Angelito was there to turn on the lights, close the curtains, heat up and serve the dinner that Angela had left for Gaspar and his friends. Angelito was even happy to run Gaspar's bath when asked. Angelito had taken it upon himself to answer the phones, answer the door, and take care of Gaspar's personal space including the Captain's Cabin, his Blue Marble Bathroom, the office and the "Haunted Room" which Gaspar decided to take over when Peugeot nearly pushed him out of his bunk in the middle of the night. He knew the day would soon come when the standard poodle would be too big to share his bunk, and that a bigger bed would be necessary for the two of them. It was the black leather and white satin Art Deco décor in the 'Haunted Room' next to the Captain's Cabin that appealed to him. The 'Haunted Room' had easy access from the Captain's Cabin, being just on the other side of the wall, which Gaspar was able to break through by creating a secret door hidden in the paneling.

With Angela and Angelito on the job, there was never a shortage of food at the Bachelor Pad, and the entire house was running ship shape like a well-oiled machine. That was exactly the way Gaspar liked it, as it left him more time to do what he liked to do … and what he liked to do right now … was exploring the Sullivan mansion with Mr. Peugeot and checking out the treasure that Jason was uncovering there.

Every day, after school, while Alex kept busy with his buddies, goofing off all over Perdido Isle, Gaspar gravitated to the old Sullivan place, where he could work with Jason, or just poke around the house on his own with Peugeot. Today was no exception. Gaspar had been a hit around the school yard with his groovy black and blue eye but when the bell rang at the end of the day, all he wanted to do was hightail it to the Sullivans'.

Whenever he got there, Rajeev was always at hand, offering tea or asking how he could help, but Gaspar found it harder to keep Rajeev busy and easier to do whatever he wanted done himself. Unlike Angelito, who had taken to La Rinconada like a duck to water, whenever Gaspar really needed Rajeev, he was either nowhere to be found or doing something inconsequential which couldn't be interrupted. But Rajeev was just a minor annoyance in a sea of promise and intrigue. Every drawer and every cupboard, and every door in the house promised to present Gaspar and Jason with who knows what kind of "trick or treat," for that's how Gaspar looked at the house lately—it was all either a trick or a treat.

Gaspar found the library to be the most compelling of the rooms, not only because of all the books, which he couldn't wait to read, but because of all the papers stuffed in the desk drawers, and filed away helter-skelter, here and there. Today his goal was to check out the safe, on his own except for Mr. Peugeot, without any distractions.

Locking the library door behind him, he took out the slip of paper that Morrie had given him the other day and started working the tumblers on the safe. He listened as the safes inner workings clicked into position, and took a deep breath as he pulled up on the levers. Using all his strength he slowly opened the heavy doors wide. What he found inside was, compared to the rest of the house, a neat, tidy, clean, and well-organized vault filled with ledgers, and envelopes, and files. "This is going to be fun," Gaspar told Peugeot, who stood up on his hind legs to get a look inside the safe too.

Grabbing a stack of folios, he carried them over to the big desk and laid them to one side. Pulling up the old oak and leather-upholstered desk chair, he made himself at home and opened the first file.

Three hours later, Peugeot was asleep at his feet and Gaspar was a lot wiser as far as the Sullivan Saga was concerned. He couldn't wait to talk with Uncle Charlie about what he'd learned.

A loud knock on the library door jolted Gaspar out of his reverie, while simultaneously waking-up Peugeot who barked angrily at the intrusion. "Gasp, it's six o'clock," Jason called through the door from the hall. "Time to lock up."

"Give me a minute, Jason, "I'll be right there." He promised. Picking up most of the ledgers, Gaspar placed them back inside the safe, closed the vault tightly and spun the lock until it clicked. The remaining book was a diary, which he put in his backpack before unlocking the door where he and Peugeot found Jason waiting for him patiently.

"Did you have a productive afternoon, Gaspar?" Jason asked solicitously.

"I've been going through the contents of the safe, and yes, what I found there was not only interesting, but productive too.

• • •

Back at La Rinconada, Angelito greeted him at the door. "May I get you a refreshment, Mr. Brown?" he asked solicitously. "Dinner will be ready whenever you would like it served." His major domo told him.

"Is Mr. Mendoza here." he asked.

"Upstairs in the television room, Sir." Angelito replied.

"Is he eating?" Gaspar chuckled.

"He has a sparkling lemonade and a platter of chips and dip, Sir." Angelito told him with glitter dancing in his bemused eyes.

"Of course he does," Gaspar laughed. "Do me a favor Angelito, run upstairs and run my bath, and then bring me a sparkling lemonade, please. You better bring some more lemonade and chips for *His Nibs* too in case he's eaten them all. We'll have dinner in an hour, Angelito. You may bring it to us on trays. We'll eat upstairs in front of the TV." Gaspar decided.

Gaspar climbed the stairs and found Alex stretched out on the sofa watching cartoons.

"Hi, Al. Did you have a good afternoon?" Gaspar asked.

"Hi, Gasp. Yeah, me and Kevin and the gang went fishing on the inland waterway and goofed around for a couple of hours. How bout you? Did you and Jason find good things at the old house?"

Gaspar knew that Alex couldn't care less about his treasure hunt, but it was nice of him to ask. "Oh yeah Al." Gaspar had plenty to tell him, but doubted that he would really listen or connect with his latest news ... but he had to tell someone. "I worked in the library at the Sullivan place this afternoon and I discovered something really interesting."

"Like what?" Alex's eyes never left the television screen.

"Just a lot of old papers, kinda interesting, but nothing earth shattering."

"That's nice." His best friend answered as he intently watched Batman bust The Joker in a series of graphic 'BOOMS, BIFFS, BANGS, AND POWS,' What'd ya learn?" came Alex's disinterested question as Angelito arrived and silently refilled Alex's lemonade, and exchanged his empty tray of chips and dip for a new one before heading into the Captain's Cabin with Gaspar's lemonade in hand.

Mr. Peugeot, who up till now had been lying quietly listening to his master's soothing voice, suddenly sat up and proceeded to roll out a long, low grumbling growl.

"What's going on, Peugeot." Gaspar asked the pooch. "Are you seeing spirits again?"

"What are you talking about?" Alex took his eyes off the set just long enough to look at the agitated dog.

"Oh, it's nothing," Gaspar assured his pal. "Every now and then … I think Peugeot sees spirits. Look at him … he's staring over at that chair, and growling, but there's nothing there." Gaspar chuckled.

"So, are you going to tell me what you found today?"

"I found a lot of ledgers in that safe in the library." Gaspar answered. "There was a journal or travel diary I guess you could call it. It was written by Tommy Sullivan, and it's all about a trip the twins took to India in 1950."

"That's nice Gasp, did they have a good time?" Alex asked not expecting an answer, still riveted to the action pack Batman scenes.

"I think they had a blast, like we just had down in Antarctica." Gaspar insisted.

"Why would they want to go to India?" Alex mumbled through a mouthful of chips.

"Because they were real adventurers." Gaspar replied. "They went in search of the lost city of Rappa, and they found it."

"What's Rappa, where's it at?" His pal never looked up from the inane cartoon he was watching.

"I don't know Al." Gaspar answered, impatiently, "I've never heard of it either I've gotta go into the library and do some research."

"More research, wouldn't you rather just watch TV with me tonight? There's a great Carole Bradie film on, you know, the one where she works in a Disco and finds true love with an ex-con south of the border."

Gaspar couldn't think of anything he'd rather not watch. "By the way, I told Angelito that we'll eat dinner on trays up here tonight … he'll be ready in an hour. I thought you might like to watch an old movie while we're at it? There's a good one, *The Seventh Adventure of Sinbad*, it's scheduled for 7:30."

"Sounds cool, what's it about?"

"Oh you know, the usual, lost cities, stolen jewels, radical terrorists, jeweled idols the whole nine yards." Gaspar gave an abbreviated synopsis.

"Okay." Alex yawned, "if you say so."

"Haven't you ever heard of *The Seventh Adventure of Sinbad?*". It stars Kerwin Mathews, Kathryn Thatcher, Richard Grant, and Alec Mango." Gaspar enthused. "It's one of those great old movies, released by Columbia in 1958 with Ray Harryhausen stop animation special effects … you know, like in *King Kong*." Gaspar waxed poetic. Wait till you see it, Al. It's a terrific movie." He hoped he'd sold the idea to his pal. At least he knew that Peugeot seemed interested as the poodle was all ears listening attentively to his master's animated description of the film.

"Sounds good," Alex commented listlessly. "Let's watch it." He said, still engrossed by the antics of Batman, Robin and The Joker.

"I'm going to clean up now, Al. I always feel so gritty after sludging around the old Sullivan place. I'll be out when dinner's served." He told Alex. By that time, Gaspar hoped, *Batman should have gotten rid of The Joker and the cartoon would be over, and the old movie about to begin.* Gaspar also wondered if Alex would ever figure out that he didn't really watch cartoons anymore.

Gaspar headed for the Captain's Cabin. As he entered, Angelito was just leaving.

"I've left your lemonade on the counter, Sir. Your bath is drawn. Is there anything else I can do for you?" he asked solicitously.

"That's all, Angelito. Thank you very much. Just let me know when dinner is served and I'll come out." He said as he removed his shoes and unbuttoned his shirt.

Alone at last, Gaspar sipped his lemonade while soaking in the tub. He let the oiled and perfumed water soak into his skin and let what he learned today soak into his brain, causing his fertile imagination to take over where fact was left behind by pure fantasy.

Eyes closed he dozed off in the relaxing hot water and he dreamed, while Peugeot snoozed on the cool marble floor. His dream was peopled by Indians in colorful saris and turbans, and he was with the Sullivan Twins and their servant, Rajeev. They traveled through a desolate countryside, riding on caparisoned camels and elephants. They came across an ancient ruin and discovered the entrance to what they thought was a tomb but which in reality turned out to be a temple dedicated to a Hindu goddess. The interior was made of carved and gilded marble and completely illuminated by blazing torches whose massive flames glittered against the gilded walls. A giant statue of a goddess stood looming over the adventurers. She had a giant gemstone imbedded in her forehead symbolizing her third eye. The next thing Gaspar knew he was climbing up onto the statue. Standing on the idol's shoulders he reached around her head, and proceeded to pry the stone loose using Uncle Charlie's Swiss Army knife, which he conveniently extracted from his khaki cargo shorts. It was a huge red stone, and filled the entire worn out leather catcher's mitt that he was suddenly wearing on his right hand. It was the same catcher's mitt he'd given to Kevin just the other day, the one with Mickey Mantle's signature on it. As he climbed down with his glittering prize, the Sullivan Twins grabbed the jewel from him just as a tribe of rag-tag natives seized him and tied him up. To Gaspar's surprise, the Sullivan Twins and Rajeev, made their escapes, running away without a thought for his predicament. Before Gaspar could figure out how he was going to get out of there, he woke up. Angelito was calling him.

"Mr. Brown, Mr. Brown, wake up Sir." Angelito called gently. When Gaspar opened his eyes, Angelito was standing next to the tub holding up a terry cloth bath sheet to wrap him in. "Dinner is served, Sir." Angelito told him, gently shaking the towel at him.

Gaspar stood up, "Thanks Angelito," he drawled sleepily. "I must have dozed off. I'll be right out, go ahead and serve Mr. Mendoza. I'm right behind you" he said, drying off.

Returning to the TV room in a terry cloth robe, he found Alex, scarfing down his dinner, while Angelito waited off to the side. "What did Angela cook for us tonight, Angelito?"

"Chicken curry, Sir." Angelito replied, placing a tray in front of him, piled high with rice and curry and dishes of condiments. "Will there be anything else, Sir?"

"Not that I can think of." Gaspar replied, looking at Alex who had nothing to offer in response.

"Come back in a while, we're going to watch an old movie. You can bring us our dessert whenever you're ready." He said, picking up his fork.

Gaspar grabbed the control and turned the TV to TCM. *The Seventh Adventure of Sinbad* was just starting.

"Feeling better?" Alex asked between forkfuls of delicious curry.

"Much better, thank you," Gaspar said. "I dozed off in the tub and had a wacky dream about India and excavating an old temple and finding a bejeweled idol." He confessed. "Al, I think there's more to the Sullivan Twins story than meets the eye. I don't think they were just recluses. I think they lived in fear for their lives and there's something in that house that they were hiding, or protecting."

"What kind of something?" Alex actually put down his fork and sounded interested in what Gaspar had to say for the first time tonight.

"I don't know, I'm not sure, but perhaps Rajeev can help me. Something tells me that he's part of the mystery." Gaspar found talking things through, out loud, with his best friend, was beneficial to getting to the bottom of solving riddles.

"Well Gasp, if I can help you in any way with your research, just ask, but you know how hopeless I am when it comes to books or papers, or anything esoteric or foreign." Alex confessed his shortcomings.

"Don't be silly Al, you know you're the first person I go to whenever I need to solve a problem." Gaspar lied, knowing Alex was completely hopeless where logical thinking was concerned. "Watch this Al. This is one of the best parts of the movie." Gaspar told his buddy.

After the scene where Sinbad found the magic cave was over, Alex piped up. "that was great, Gasp. If you find out anything critically important about Rappa, please let me know at once. I'm interested in everything you're interested in, buddy. If Rappa is anything like this Sinbad movie, you can count me in."

"You were actually listening to me when I mentioned Rappa?" Gaspar marveled.

"Of course I was listening. You think I can't do two things at once? Give me a break, Gasp. Just because I was making sure that Batman clobbered The Joker, doesn't mean I wasn't listening to every word you said," Alex assured him.

Gaspar was impressed, from now on he wouldn't be so quick to discount his pals mental capacities. He was also pleased that Alex was into the movie. He appreciated AL's friendship, but also felt that the less Al knew about Rappa or any other esoteric subject the better, after all... that's what made Al ... Al.

• • •

It had been a pleasant evening. The curry dinner with condiments couldn't have been better, and the chocolate sundaes Angelito concocted for them really hit the spot. The minute the movie ended, Alex said goodnight and headed back to his parents apartment over the stables. Gaspar on the other hand went directly to the library. It was 9:30 but as far as he was concerned there was no time like the present for doing research. Grabbing the diary from his backpack he went through the secret panel in the Captain's Cabin which connected with the balcony that wrapped around the library. Descending the spiral staircase he walked over to the main doors and locked them. Feeling secure, he went straight to work.

Going to the "India" section of book shelves which had been arranged by subject, he pulled down several large volumes filled with old black and white photos. Spreading them out on the big center table, he pulled up a chair and starting turning pages. He discovered cities and towns he'd never heard of and names and titles of Maharajas, princes, and Indian notables that he'd only dreamed of. Photographs of palaces and elephants caparisoned with rich silks and embroideries and gigantic jewels, filled the pages. Chapters on festivals and religious ceremonies conjured up a land of mystery and pageantry he longed to see firsthand. He was browsing through the third book in the pile he'd plucked from the shelves when the word *Rappa*, jumped out at him from the old yellowed pages. What he read, astounded him.

The lost city of Rappa, was presumably located in the middle of the sub-continent, located in the center of a lake, surrounded by thick jungle. Legend placed the lost city somewhere between *the Himalayas and the Arabian Sea*. Running over to consult Uncle Charlie's magnificent bronze and mahogany mounted globe, he saw that *somewhere between the Himalayas and the Arabian Sea* was a vast expanse of land. How would he ever find it? And then he got to thinking. If the Sullivan Twins found it, why couldn't he? He just had to use rational thinking … but where to begin?

Peugeot ran over to the sofa by the fireplace barking like crazy.

"Uncle Charlie, are you around? I need to talk with you." Gaspar called out hoping for an answer.

"Right over here, Gaspar." Uncle Charlie's friendly voice reverberated from the coral velvet sofa near the fireplace. "I have no peace when that *French Busy Body Poodle* of yours is around." He bemoaned Peugeot's ability to spot him, even when he was invisible.

"Have you been there all the time?" Gaspar asked, as the old ghost sat up from a reclining position on the sofa and showed his head and shoulders over the back of the upholstered furniture.

"Yes, I've been having a lie-down waiting for you to ask me about, *The Lost City of Rappa*." He chuckled.

"You know what I'm looking for?" Gaspar couldn't believe Uncle Charlie's ability to find out everything he was doing without the slightest effort.

"Don't get excited, Gasp. I was in the TV room listening to every word you said while you and Alex were having dinner," the ghost confessed with a shrug. "So tell me, what's this all about, and what and *Where The Blooming Diplodocus*, is Rappa?

"Well I found a mention of it in this diary written by Tommy Sullivan." Gaspar held up the book he'd found in the safe. "It mentions an adventure the twins had in India in 1950," Gaspar said, flipping through the diary he'd found at the mansion. "Look, it's right here." Gaspar pointed out the mention of Rappa in Tommy Sullivans' hand writing. Apparently, it was a legendary city, like Atlantis or something like that. It says so right here, in this old volume I've just pulled off our shelves. It's was a secret place where the Hindus put all their most important treasures and religious objects in advance of the Muslim pillaging. The Hindus wanted to safeguard their treasure from the Moghul invaders and I guess the guys who did the hiding, were wiped out in the process and their secret hiding place was lost forever, or almost forever. According to this book, they left a lot of people behind in Rappa to take care of the place, but the secret location of Rappa was subsequently lost forever and it seems no one has ever stumbled upon it since." Gaspar told Uncle Charlie breathlessly.

"Nobody but the un-professional Sullivan Twins you mean." Uncle Charlie let him know that he was not only informed but one step ahead of him.

"You've known about the Sullivans' adventures all this time and never told me?" Gaspar asked accusingly.

"Not at all, I just happened to be reading that diary over your shoulder this afternoon while you and *Fido* here, were at the mansion." Uncle Charlie confessed.

"Do you do that a lot, uncle?" Gaspar was a bit alarmed and slightly annoyed. "It's not that I mind, but I would much rather have shared the diary with you than to have been … spied on," Gaspar groused. "I mean, really Uncle Charlie, I'd like a little privacy. It's not that I don't want you around all the time, or that your barging into my bathroom for a chat now and then doesn't bother me, but if you're there, please let me know."

"Apologies all around dear boy, I feel miserable about not making my presence known, but you see, I wasn't the only one spying on you this afternoon, so I didn't want to give myself away or you either, by letting you know."

"Someone else spying on me! What are you talking about?" Gaspar was thunderstruck.

"Your buddy, Rajeev. He was watching you from a spy hole drilled through the ceiling, right over the Sullivan library desk. I don't know if it's his special spy hole, or if it was created by one of the Sullivan Twins, but I do know that he was up there watching you." Uncle Charlie insisted.

"I don't like hearing this uncle." Gaspar couldn't wrap his head around this new revelation. "What do you suggest I do, going forward?" The teenager asked the old ghost.

"Do exactly what you did tonight, bring any important documents home with you and lock them up in your own secret vault, upstairs." Charlie instructed him, referring to the vault Gaspar had installed in the secret compartment between the Captain's Cabin and the library balcony, back when he'd first discovered Gasparilla's treasure.

"Shall I confront Rajeev, or just let it slide?" he asked his elder.

"Don't rock the boat, Gasp." Uncle Charlie guided his young friend. "Let it ride, but keep a sharp lookout. I think Rajeev is harmless, and wildly eccentric, but after what I witnessed today, I think his actions bear watching," Uncle Charlie warned.

"Okay, uncle, I hear you loud and clear. Thanks for the advice."

"So what do you know about Rappa that I don't?" Uncle Charlie asked.

"Well, I made some notes this afternoon, which I have here." Gaspar picked up a handful of papers off the desk and proceeded to read his notes to Uncle Charlie. "Let's see … from what I could gather from the diary, they found the lost city in the Indus River Valley, which was home to some of the oldest civilizations on earth. Have you ever been there, uncle?

"You know how much I love India, Gasp. I've been there a hundred times, and I've visited a lot of old ruined cities too, but I don't know anything about Rappa. So fire away!"

The Indus Valley's got China to the north and north-east and the Thar Desert on the east." Gaspar walked over to the globe and pointed this out to Uncle Charlie. "The Hindu Kush with its vast desert lies to the west and north west, over here," he pointed to the globe, "and as you can see here, the Arabian Sea and Indian Ocean to the south, complete the boundaries of the Indus Valley." Gaspar described the lay of the land while pointing out the features on Uncle Charlie's globe. "It says in that old book on the table that there are also thick jungles in the Indus growing along the banks of the Ganges." Gaspar told Uncle Charlie, walking back to the books on the table. Apparently, the valley was so rich that it's people thrived and ultimately controlled more than 500,000 square miles of territory which is more than the ancient Egyptians or even the Mesopotamians ever controlled." Gaspar finished his geography and history lesson with a flourish. 'I think that whatever the Sullivan twins found in the Indus River Valley, was most probably Harappan."

"HARAPPAN? What's that?" Uncle Charlie asked incredulously.

Harappan is the name of the culture that thrived in the area around 3500 BC. I think what the twins keep referring to as Rappa, might be in the same vicinity as the present archeological digs of Harappa or Hampi, depending on which historian or archeologist you read. Whatever the name of the city was, it's known that at some critical point, it became naturally cut off from all others in India by its unique geography and the changing flow of the Ganges river, which is fed by summer rains and winter runoff from the Himalayas. It is the Ganges that feeds the lake in which the island where the city of Rappa, was located."

"It shouldn't be too hard to find an island in the middle of the Ganges river." Uncle Charlie brightened considering how easy this was going to be. "There can't be that many of them to choose from," he insisted.

"There's a strong possibility uncle that it's not an island anymore. It's highly possible that the river changed course around the island, or that the river silted up one side of the island, turning it into more of a bump along the river front. Today it might just look like a bump of riverside land with water lapping along three sides of it for example. There's also the possibility that the entire place is under water now, the river having covered it completely!" Gaspar explained logically.

Like I said, Gasp. I've been there. The Indus Valley is a veritable oasis. The river provides rich silt to grow rice, wheat, fruits and vegetables and also cotton. Just like the Nile does in Egypt," Uncle Charlie finished.

"And grazing lands too for cattle." Gaspar added, "and plenty of fresh water, all of which are just as important now as they were back then." Gaspar interjected. "It makes you wonder, Uncle ... with all of this natural wealth, why the city would have been abandoned, and ultimately forgotten? Gaspar shook his head.

"Maybe like you said, the river changed course once too often, flooding the land forcing the people to leave, or maybe there were destructive earthquakes?" Uncle Charlie offered as another excuse for the mysterious end to such a rich civilization. "When you think about it, Gasp, Cities are just as mortal as their human occupants." Uncle Charlie philosophized.

"The most important temple in Rappa was *The Masilamanai Nathar Koil* temple." Gaspar informed him, reading the information from his notes.

"Never heard of it!" Uncle Charlie dismissed the information as unimportant. "What kind of a temple is that?" Charlie asked unimpressed.

"It's also listed right here," Gaspar pointed to the open book on the table. "That temple was a big deal back in the 13th century." Gaspar insisted, "It says here that the temple was under the patronage of the Chola Kings, who ruled the place with an iron fist when the Tamils were in charge." He read from the book on the table. "That would have been before the river flooded and washed the whole city away except for the buildings made of stone, like the temple for example." Gaspar assumed trying to separate fact from fiction. "That legendary flood, covered most of the place with mud and silt, but that was only one flood, legend has it that Rappa suffered flooding more than five times in five centuries." Gaspar filled Uncle Charlie in on the legendary history of Rappa. "It says here that it was the capital of the Vijaynagar Empire, and ruled by four dynasties, Sangama, Saluva, Tuluva and Aravidu." Gaspar read the details from the open book. "The princes who ruled the place built more than 500 monuments to their gods, and the place was so rich from trade that it was the envy of all its neighbors causing jealousy and ultimately war with the Deccan Muslims who wanted to take it over at any cost. In 1565 according to history, the city was pillaged by the Muslims over a six-month siege before finally being abandoned by the Hindus. Apparently, after the Hindus left, the Moghul conquerors could find no trace of the storied treasure." Gaspar's notes were thin, but the book completed whatever was missing.

"Makes you wonder," Uncle Charlie mused, "Where they hid their loot?"

"In their journal the twins describe the area where they found whatever it was they were seeking. They write about a spectacular setting dominated by the Ganges River, surrounded by craggy hills and massive boulders and miles of undulating terrain, where lush green palm groves, banana plantations and rice fields grew wild. It is in this setting that they discovered whatever was left of a temple they called Vithala. Whatever they found there was such a secret that they didn't dare mention it in writing, not even in their own diary, but alluded to it only in a roundabout way," Gaspar explained.

"So far you've only mentioned two temples," Uncle Charlie pointed out. "For such a rich and important 'Lost City,' only two temples seem like slim pickings."

"Oh there were more mentioned in the diary. Be patient uncle, I'm trying to sort this out." Gaspar begged the old boy as he looked through his notes. "They also mention the Kizhthali Shiva Temple. They write here that Pliny, the ancient Roman chronicler, mentions these two temples, and states that ancient Rome traded with the Indus bringing them gold in return for black pepper, calling the city of Rappa 'the first emporium of India, full of important monuments and religious sites.'" He read from the diary.

"Pliny! That's saying a lot, Gasp." Uncle Charlie was impressed.

"I looked Rappa up on Google, uncle, and Google says that Rappa is India's most mysterious lost city, which archeologists the world over dream of discovering and excavating someday. Well the twins' diary is dated 1950, so apparently they got there before anyone else did." Gaspar was satisfied with the dates. "Google also mentions that if Rappa is ever found, it would surely hold a blend of Nagara and Dravidian architectural forms representing a high point of the eclectic style of art that developed under the Chalukya dynasty." Gaspar quoted. "Unlike when the Sullivans were there, today Rappa would be a UNESCO world heritage site, like the excavated site at Hampi, which holds a stunning complex of several 8th century Shiva temples and a Jain sanctuary. Archeologists dream of finding the fabled Temple of Virupaksha, or the Pampapati Temple, dedicated to Lord Shiva and his consort, the local goddess Pampa who is also mentioned by Pliny."

"Pliny said all that? It's mind boggling, Gasp! You're joking aren't you?" Uncle Charlie scratched his head.

"No, uncle I'm not. Pliny wrote about the temple built by Queen Lokamahadevi to commemorate her

husband's victory over the Pallava Kings of Kanchi."
Gaspar knew he was butchering the names with his
American pronunciation, but was certain that he had the
history down-pat as he read from his notes.

"Sounds like the place might be worth finding, Gasp.
What are your plans? Will you be heading to India next?"
Uncle Charlie wanted to know.

"I like the way you think, Uncle, but no, I have no
plans to visit India, at least not in the near future." Gaspar
told him.

"So what do you think the Sullivans found there?
They certainly didn't bring back an entire temple, Gasp."
Uncle Charlie wondered.

"It had to be something small and precious." Gaspar
decided. "You know Uncle, this was a rich ancient city,
full of temples to various Hindu gods. I think they found
jewels or a jewel of immense monetary and historical
value. If they did steal a religious jewel, perhaps it was
cursed. That could account for the twins miserable
existence on Perdido Isle." Gaspar speculated.

"It's not a bad theory, Gasp, but have you any proof
that the Hindus in the Indus Valley were that rich back
then? You know, rich enough to supply their Gods with
magnificent jewels for example." Uncle Charlie wanted
facts.

"Uncle Charlie, these dudes weren't any different
than the other civilizations spread out across India or
even other civilizations around the world. The Indus

people worshiped fire. They were rich enough to build altars to fire, and temples to fire, and what is the 'fire stone', Uncle? The mighty ruby, king of gemstones which the Indians called Ratnaraj. Are you following my thinking, uncle?" Gaspar asked with flashing eyes. "In their diary the Sullivans describe various artifacts that they found in the fire temples including seals, bangles, terracotta objects and figurines, bricks, grinders and stone balls. They described the fire temple as rich with treasure but only mention the most mundane items." Makes you wonder doesn't it?" Gaspar asked his older and wiser relative.

"I need more than speculation, Gasp. Give me facts." Uncle Charlie insisted.

"According to Google search, and we know that's not always accurate, Rappa was first discovered by a British explorer named Charles Masson in 1820 when he stumbled across some mysterious ruins and brick mounds. This was the first evidence of the lost city of Rappa, all of which was forgotten until 36 years later in 1856 when railway engineers found more bricks and carted them off before continuing their railway construction, and again the city was forgotten. Then, according to their diary, the Sullivan twins say that they found Rappa and took home treasure from it. Today archeologists hope to find Rappa, and think that when they do, it will be like a window looking in on one of the oldest civilization in the world." Gaspar informed his doubting uncle.

"Facts, Gasp. I want to hear about some real treasure please." Charlie insisted, again .

"In their diary, the Sullivans mention artefacts, like beads, jewelry and pottery. Today archeologists speculate that if they could just find it, Rappa would be one of the richest digs on earth. Based on other digs in the Indus Valley, jewelry and jeweled objects are the most commonly found artifacts . Apparently in the good old days, both men and women, throughout the Indus Valley adorned themselves, with ornaments wrought in precious metals and gemstones." Gaspar was enthusiastic, but Uncle Charlie was still skeptical.

This is the best part, Uncle. According to legend, the people of Rappa worshiped a mother goddess. Archeologists have recovered a large number of mother goddess figurines from almost every excavated site in the Indus Valley which suggests that other mother goddess worship was widespread and popular, and the people of Rappa would no doubt have been involved in the same beliefs. Where there's a mother goddess ... or a lady ... there's got to be jewels." Gaspar put two and two together. "Remember the big battle with the Moghuls I told you about? Well, lore has it that it was devastating to the city of Rappa. When the invaders couldn't find the Hindu treasure, they massacred the entire population. In other areas of the Indus, archeologists have found dozens of human remains dating from the time of the Moghul take-over. In one street alone, at Urdu, they uncovered 44 scattered skeletons, sprawled on the pavement. It's been speculated that death came suddenly to the victims who were obviously running away from terror. One group included a father, mother and child who were found still holding hands. All of these victims were flattened to the ground lying in contorted positions, surrounded by layers of rubble, ash and debris. The Moghuls must have slain them before burning the town and ripping it to the ground in search of hidden treasure."

"So Gasp, throw me a bone. Of all those magnificent temples, which one would have been the richest?" Uncle Charlie cut to the chase.

"Okay, Uncle. Archeologists have already found temples in other digs dedicated to Shiva, Vishnu, Shakti, Ganesh and Hanuman and also to those of all their other forms. Dozens of temples." Gaspar made his point. "Take Shiva for example, it wouldn't have been unusual for her to have a huge precious stone symbolizing her third eye imbedded in her forehead, in proportion to the size of her statue which would have been in proportion to the architecture dedicated to her. Where do you think the Daya-ye Noor Diamond came from?" He asked his doubting uncle. "It means 'Sea of Light' and was mined at Golconda and later found set into a statue of the Goddess Shiva. It's now part of the Iranian crown jewels, but was stolen in the 18th century and sold to the Persians on the open market."

"I'm impressed," Uncle Charlie chuckled, his eyes sparkling avariciously.

"There were also temples to Vishnu and his incarnations as Krishna and Rama. The famous Black Orlov Diamond is also called 'The Eye of Brahma'. Supposedly The Black Orlov was stolen from a statue of Vishnu way back in the 17th century in its original 195 carat form." Gaspar said.

Before Uncle Charlie could get a word in edgewise, Gaspar continued, "History tells us that the people of Rappa revered Shakti, the mother goddess, including her other forms as Durga, Kali, Lakshmi and Saraswati. If the Sullivans did find a jewel it could have been one of hers. The original form of the Hope Diamond was supposedly the stolen third eye of a sculpted statue of the goddess Shakti.

"I like where you're going with this, Gasp. Tell me more." Uncle Charlie encouraged.

"I'm sure you've heard of The Koh-I-Noor Diamond or "Mountain of Light?"

"Yes of course it's one of the most famous precious stones on earth." Charlie replied.

"As legend has it, the massive 186 carat stone was stolen from the forehead of a statue of the Hindu god Krishna. A spoil of war, that huge diamond steadily passed among Hindu, Mughal, Persian, Afghan, and Sikh rulers before being recut to 109 carats when it was added to the British crown jewels in 1877.

"And so?" Uncle Charlie raised an eyebrow.

"And so ... it was in the news not so many months ago that archeologists have recently uncovered, in the Indus Valley, the lost Temple of Agneya dedicated to Agneya, daughter of the fire God Agni. What they found there is a 20-foot-tall statue of the goddess carved in red sandstone with a gaping hole in her forehead big enough to pitch a baseball through." Gaspar looked at Charlie knowingly. "Get it?"

"And so ...?"

"And so, I think at last, they may have found the lost city of Rappa, and I also think that the Sullivans may have found an enormous red rock and have hidden it inside their mansion right here on Perdido Isle." Gaspar fantasized.

"Hmmm... okay, let's see if we can find it." Uncle Charlie was game.

Mr. Peugeot was game too, jumping up, he started barking furiously in Uncle Charlie's direction.

"Someone wants to go out." He told Gaspar with one eyebrow cocked. "I think it's me." He joked as he dematerialized right in front of the barking dog.

TREASURE HUNT

AYS TURNED INTO WEEKS AND WEEKS INTO MONTHS AS JASON AND HIS CREW EXCAVATED AND SEPARATED the trash from the treasure. In all, Jason figured they'd removed four tons of trash from inside the house. Each day he presented Gaspar and Mr. Peugeot with new revelations, one more interesting than the next. Rajeev had shown them the tunnels connecting the main house to the carriage house, the guest house, and the pool pavilions. Those tunnels too were crammed with boxes and piles of old junk. Hubcaps, old radios, tube televisions, dozens of old telephones, doorknobs, hinges, piles of old window screens, broken chairs, wicker baskets, dozens of lamps, and even more worn out, torn and bent old lampshades. There were boxes of tassels, and costume jewelry and barrels of old shoes, which Peugeot especially liked sniffing and walking sticks which Gaspar looked through with appreciation. There were pyramids of old hats, from bowlers, to Tyroleans, straw hats to silk top hats, all in various states of disrepair. When the second-floor hallways had been cleared of their collections of balls of yarn, old lace tablecloths, dozens of telephone books, crates of old soda pop bottles, and paper bags containing just pencils, Gaspar, and Peugeot who never left his side, could finally see inside the various bedrooms.

"The bedrooms were typically furnished with Grand Rapids-type matching suites of chests of drawers, mirrors, chaises and arm chairs, dressing tables, cheval glasses, and bedsteads. The wall to wall carpets had been laid, and Gaspar directed that they be removed and thrown out.

The twins had determined that clothing should be the domain of the bedrooms and clothes are what Gaspar, Peugeot and Jason found there. What they discovered while excavating the bedrooms was revealing. One room was filled with men's clothes: from Saville Row sartorial, to J. C. Penney threadbare; top coats, sport coats, dinner jackets, three-piece suites, seersucker suits, golfing togs, tennis togs, swim trunks and all manner of bathing costumes as well as underwear in all sizes from tiny to enormous. Peugeot grabbed a pair of Brooks Brothers boxer shorts and ran around the room with them in his mouth before proceeding to rip them to shreds. There were also shirts: dress shirts, polo shirts, long sleeved shirts and short sleeved shirts, t-shirts, and wife beaters, the array of men's shirts was practically endless.

"Jason, there are more clothes here, than even Uncle Charlie had in his closets." Gaspar laughed after seeing the mountain of smelly old clothes. "Unless you think some of this stuff is museum worthy, I suggest you should send it all to the Goodwill, sooner than later," Gaspar suggested, "before Peugeot tears it all to shreds." Gaspar laughed.

Another bedroom held women's clothing: evening clothes, cocktail dresses, shirt dresses, housecoats, moth-eaten mink coats and stoles, as well as capes with the same array in sable, leopard, monkey fur, and even zebra. There were slacks, and swimsuits and bikinis, some just tops and some just bottoms. Gaspar couldn't believe all the different types and sizes of ladies underwear they found there or why girls needed so many underpinnings. Skirts, blouses, pajamas, nightgowns, robes, and slippers, and shoes, mountains and mountains of shoes for every occasion ... but that wasn't all. Peugeot loved shoes, the smellier the better. Gaspar nearly fell over laughing when he looked down and saw the goofy pup with a high heeled pump in a leopard skin pattern dangling from his drooling mouth.

Other bedrooms held children's clothes for both boys and girls. Clothes to rival even those made for adults which they'd found in the other rooms. There was also a nursery, or what might have been a nursery, full of infant wear, and toys—so many toys—mostly broken or in need of repair. There were dolls of every type from valuable antique French dolls to more recent plastic monstrosities. Peugeot dropped the shoe when he found a red, rubber ball to push around the room with his nose while Gaspar and Jason headed for one of the bathrooms.

What they found there was even crazier. Every surface in every bathroom was stacked with bottles. Perfume bottles, some in fancy crystal or molded glass, and others only glass. Pill bottles abounded, both in glass and plastic. Along with all the bottles were mixed tubes of creams and ointments, as well as dried out tubes of toothpaste, and jars and jars of hair pomade and dried out beauty creams. Lipsticks, some in fancy jeweled cases, others in simple plastic tubes were legion. Hundreds of boxes of lipstick, never used or ever opened, the most amusing being the ones labeled 'Kiss Proof'. According to Jason, the bottles labeled Nuit de Noel were of a rare perfume, as were the dozens of unopened bottles of Poiret-Nuit de Chine, too. Gaspar opened a bottle of the rare scent and put it to his nose. When Peugeot jumped up to see what all the fuss was about, Gaspar held the bottle for Peugeot to sniff. Both men howled with laughter as Peugeot ran out of the room, barking furiously, before rolling on the floor trying to wipe the smell out of his nostrils, onto the carpet. Turning their attention to the bathtub they discovered it full to overflowing with cosmetics, and razors—new, used and rusty—and electric beauty gadgets for curling hair, or smoothing wrinkles, or drying or cutting hair.

"You're not gonna have a lot of fun with these bathrooms." Gaspar told Jason.

"Tell me about it, Gasp. This is only the tip of the iceberg. They're all like this, filled to the gills with trash and every now and then, some treasure."

"There's some really interesting stuff in here, but separating it all out is gonna be a lot of work." Gaspar noted. "If you'd like some help, maybe Peugeot and I can come by and help you one of these afternoons." Gaspar offered.

"I can use all the help I can get." Jason confessed, "Don't think I'm daunted by any of this, Gasp … I'm having the time of my life over here, but if you want to pitch in, it's fine with me, although something tells me that Peugeot's not going to like going through the perfumes much." Jason chucked as Peugeot stuck his curly head around the corner of the door to make sure the coast was clear of any opened perfume bottles.

· · ·

Every day for the next two weeks, Gaspar raced after school to visit the old Sullivan place. He was a man on a mission, *a secret mission*, to find out what the Sullivan twins were hiding in their house, and what it was that they were so scared of losing. Rajeev greeted him at the door each day, and attempted to make himself useful. Ever since Uncle Charlie told him that Rajeev might not be trustworthy, Gaspar felt like he was walking on eggshells whenever the Indian servant was near. In order to insure his privacy, whenever he arrived at the house, he would instruct Rajeev to go with La Mar in the car to run a hair-brained errand he'd concocted. He'd given La Mar strict instructions to drive Rajeev around *the long way*, in order to keep the foreign devil out of his hair for as long as possible.

Except for Jason, who kept to himself cataloging the good stuff while continuing to throw out tons of garbage, Gaspar liked being alone in the house. He enjoyed the freedom to measure each room, searching for hidden panels, or corridors between rooms, hoping to find something about the house that had been overlooked. Maybe if I'm lucky, I might even discover a secret room, he thought to himself. Hope always sprung eternal in Gaspar's heart. In order to concentrate on the house, Gaspar had taken a leave of absence from all of his favorite sporting activities. He missed goofing off with the guys, but he knew that if he was to solve the mystery of *The House of Mystery*, he had to knuckle down and concentrate.

It had been weeks since Gaspar and Uncle Charlie had discussed the ancient lost city of Rappa. Today was no different than yesterday, except that Mr. Peugeot was spending the day at the groomer's. When Gaspar entered the house he felt less than confident realizing there was no end in sight as far as his search was concerned. In the past week with Peugeot by his side he'd already scoured the two guest houses, as well as the underground tunnels leading to them from the basement of the mansion. He and Peugeot had already been over each of the rooms in the main house with a fine-toothed comb, but to no avail. Nothing had presented itself to him or his pup which would constitute a secret hiding place for treasure. Today, there were only two stones left unturned, the attic of the mansion and its basement.

The basement was a gloomy proposition and Gaspar wished that Peugeot was there to keep him company. It was amazing he thought, how much he relied on Peugeot for company and affection since his mom had moved out. Bringing his thoughts back to the job at hand, Gaspar decided to tackle the basement first. The same door and flight of stairs that serviced the tunnels, also serviced the basement. Jason had already cleared the area, and unlocked the door. Flipping on the lights, the huge subterranean room became instantly bathed in bright white light. The idea of a secret room being accessible from this room seemed unlikely, but Gaspar searched its every corner with a powerful flashlight in hand just in case. There was one thing that he was sure of. There were no trap doors leading to any hidden rooms underneath the basement's dusty cement floor. The walls were solid poured concrete, and there were no other doors in or out of the basement except for the doors at the end of each tunnel connecting the basement to the guest house, the pool pavilions, and the carriage house. Having already searched through the tunnels several times hoping to find a hidden door, Gaspar finally gave up and decided to return upstairs.

Standing at the intersection where the two tunnels lead left and right, towards the guest house and pool pavilions, and the third tunnel straight ahead to the carriage house he suddenly came to the realization that he hadn't ever seen the second floor of the carriage house. Turning on his heels, he decided that the upstairs of the carriage house would be his next search. Arriving at the end of the tunnel, he found a circular staircase leading upwards, and he climbed it. At the top, a paneled door opened into what would have been the grooms' quarters on the second floor above the stables. Reaching the second-floor hallway, he looked to his left and saw the staircase that led down towards the door that led to the motor court, which was still nailed shut with heavy boards across it. The hall had four other doors. He opened the first door cautiously, not wanting to trip another of the twins' lethal booby traps. One by one, he opened each door. Determining that none of them were rigged or booby trapped, he breathed a sigh of relief.

The first room he looked into turned out to be a very small kitchen. As he stepped onto the filthy linoleum, black roaches scattered seeking shelter under the baseboards. The sordid sink was also crawling with vermin. Old, unwashed dishes caked with grime were stacked in the sink and across the stained counter. The grease-spattered stove held rusting black iron pots and pans. He noticed that there was no refrigerator, just an old-fashioned ice box whose door was hanging ajar on a single hinge. The contents of the outdated contraption were the remains of long rotten provisions. Gaspar gagged, and turned away, quickly closing the kitchen door behind him.

The next door he opened revealed a small old-fashioned bathroom. Another disgusting mess, Gaspar thought. The old claw-footed tub was rusted and exhibited a six inches wide, brownish yellow ring around it, Even worse, a layer of dried out mud, or worse, covered the tub's bottom. It wouldn't surprise me if the plumbing up here is backed up. Gaspar thought. The old wall-mounted sink was in no better condition and from the look of it, threatened to fall off the wall any minute. The toilet was an old-fashioned contraption, with a box hanging overhead on the wall with a long rusty pull-chain flush. He was thankful that the lid was down so he wouldn't have to see the condition of the bowl. He couldn't believe the dirt and grime on the old ceramic octagon-shaped tile floor and he took note of all the rusted, old-chrome towel bars, hooks and fixtures. Gaspar thought about the poor workman destined to clean up the *Puking, Mangled, Mewling, Mess* and wondered how could Rajeev have lived in such squalor for so many years?

When he opened the next door along the hallway, a sickly-sweet smell of rot filled his nostrils. What he discovered inside was a long dormitory with four iron beds lined up in a row. Three of the beds were unmade, with old, stained, ticking-covered mattresses and old yellowed bed pillows laying limp and flat on top. The fourth bed had linens, but was un-made. It was a pile of filthy, rumpled sheets, blankets and towels, he cringed at his assessment. Between each bed stood a dusty, white painted metal night stand, each with a shelf and a drawer. On top of each of these was an old rusty student lamp with a dusty green glass shade. At the foot of each bed was a white enameled metal trunk and standing across from each bed, lined up like sentinels, were four tall narrow lockers, each placed next to a metal desk. Each desk was outfitted with another student lamp and its own metal chair. Impulsively, Gaspar walked down the narrow room, opening each trunk and each locker one by one. They were all completely empty. He also stepped between the beds, and opened the drawers of the night stands, but all were bare.

Reaching the last bed at the end of the room near the grimy window, Gaspar opened the locker across from it and found a collection of, old worn-out Indian costumes, mostly yellowed, thread-bare Khurta pajamas in what had been white cotton, but were now stained and discolored. Also hanging there were several long coats embroidered with tarnished gold thread and studded with mirrors or glass jewels. This is Rajeev's room, Gaspar told himself. All of a sudden, he felt he was trespassing, but he continued his search opening the trunk at the end of the bed. A stale sickly-sweet smell emanating from the trunk made him realize that if this was Rajeev's trunk, he hadn't opened it in years. Inside the trunk he found books written in an Arabic or Hindi script, old embroidered shoes as well as tooled leather slippers, and papers handwritten in a strange middle-eastern script. There were also old maps of India, and the United States, and another map only of Florida. These were all worn, creased, and torn and looked to have been used repeatedly over many years, but not recently. Next, Gaspar opened the drawer of the night stand, only to discover paper and pencils, some scribbled notes again written in Arabic or what he supposed might be Hindustani, a bottle of aspirin, and a book he thought might be of a religious nature. At the back of the drawer, he found a box of bullets and a revolver. Picking up the gun, he discovered that it was loaded. With a shiver, he put it back exactly as he'd found it. The desk was neatly laid out, almost like a shrine. There was a printed picture of a Hindu goddess, several candles in colored glass holders, another religious type of book and more papers written in foreign script. Subconsciously, Gaspar took out his phone and snapped a few pictures. I wonder what language this is written in?

Gaspar had seen enough and decided he'd intruded on Rajeev's private space too long. With a definite feeling of guilt, he quickly left the room and closed the door behind him. He felt like a trespasser, somehow dirty, and a little bit ashamed that he'd snooped. The only thing he felt good about was getting the funky smell out of his nostrils once he was back in the hallway.

The last door he walked through opened into a large sitting room overlooking the motor court. Gaspar stepped to the window and realized that this was the place where he'd first laid eyes on Rajeev so many weeks ago. He shuddered recalling how scared he and his pals had been that day thinking Rajeev was actually the Devil. Looking around the room, the words, a tidy mess, came to mind. Rather than being arranged logically for comfort or conversation, old broken-down furniture was scattered here and there at random. Dirty, dusty and dingy, he thought, were the catch words for the entire apartment. There was a large broken-down, old sofa, the pillows not having been fluffed since the last person had plopped down on them, and a large table desk, covered with papers, again written in foreign script. There was a little altar arranged on the desktop with candles that had burned down to stubs, and images of pagan gods or idols, none of which Gaspar recognized. There was also a very large, and very old key with a tag attached to it. The tag read: MAUSOLEUM, in a thick scrawl. Gaspar put the key in his pocket … for later and continued looking around the disarranged room. Here and there were more dirty dishes, old books and torn magazines covering the tabletops. It was a completely closed atmosphere, *that hadn't been lived in for a long time*, he thought.

"Hadn't been lived in for a long time?" Gaspar said aloud the words he'd been thinking.

All of a sudden, he wondered where does Rajeev actually live? It was obvious *the Hindu isn't sleeping here.* Gaspar had no idea what made him think that. *There's that messy bed by the window in the dormitory, but the kitchen and the whole place is such a pig sty, no one could live in such squalor, but perhaps it's better than what Rajeev was used to in India?*

For whatever reason, he walked back to the dormitory, opening the door, he was hit by that sweet smell of rot. Without any trepidation he sauntered over to the bed under the window. Reaching down he pulled back the rumpled bed clothes and couldn't believe what he saw.

The sheets and mattress were covered in splotches of dried blood, the color of rust. Taking a corner of the soiled bed clothes between his thumb and index finger he gingerly pulled back the sheets. He could hear them separating as the dried blood sticking them together, crackled apart. He was sickened by what he saw, and wondered, *What exactly had taken place here?*

Gaspar made his way back to the main house, more confused than ever. He turned around and went outside again hoping the fresh air would clear his troubled mind. Strolling through the tangled garden, he approached the guest house and went inside. The main room had windows on two sides. Without stopping he walked across the room and out the French doors opposite where he had entered. He now found himself in a previously unexplored garden where the Sullivan Family's gothic-style mausoleum stood. It was a solemn structure, forlorn, and abandoned with a high pointed roof, and spires in each corner. Gaspar marched up to the linen-fold paneled door and taking the rusty, old key out of his pocket, thrust it into the lock. Turning it to the right, the lock clicked open. Using his shoulder he pushed the heavy door inwards while the rusty hinges screamed, "KEEP OUT!" The stench of decay filled his nostrils, a putrid smell, so ripe it took all of Gaspar's willpower not to puke. Grabbing his handkerchief he covered his nose and mouth before stepping inside the rank interior, leaving the door ajar behind him.

After a while Gaspar's eyes adjusted to the dim light. Turning on his flashlight, he took in his dismal surroundings. The interior was a mess, cobwebs covered the windows and hung from the ceiling, and rat droppings were everywhere. Shining his light around the crypt he could see that it was a large room, with shadowy alcoves on each wall holding benches built into deep niches.

Down the middle of the room, six extravagantly carved white marble sarcophagi were lined up. Starting with the two most lavishly carved tombs in the center, Gaspar spotted the name, Sir George Sullivan inscribed onto its lid. To the right of Sir George's tomb was a similarly, but not identically carved marble tomb. Shining his light over the lid he illuminated the inscription of Lady Ida Sullivan. Gaspar already knew from what Uncle Charlie had told him that the unhappy couple were buried side by side at their castle in the Yungas valley of Bolivia, so he assumed that these two marble crypts were empty and merely ornamental. Next to these on the left were two other white marble sarcophagi engraved with the names of Edward and Heddie Sullivan. Gaspar wracked his brain but couldn't remember if Uncle Charlie had told him that the parents of the Sullivan twins were buried here on Perdido Isle or in Switzerland? To the left of their grandparents, the next two white marble sarcophagi could only be those of the unhappy Sullivan Twins, Tommy and Timmy, entombed here for eternity. From what he could see, they were identical in the way they were carved, twin tombs for twin brothers carved with the names Thomas Sullivan and Timothy Sullivan. Standing next to Timmy's tomb propped up against the wall was a fancy wooden coffin lined in imperial yellow silk, replete with tassel-trimmed curtained windows. Flashing his light inside Gaspar saw the grizzly,grinning cadaver. It was Timmy, sitting up, his knees doubled under his chin just as Uncle Charlie had described him, surrounded by dead flowers arranged in blue and white Chinese vases set onto fancy built-in shelves on each side of him.

There was also central altar, decorated with tarnished old silver candelabra, which seemed to be listing to the left, their discolored candles skewing in all directions. Above the altar an old master's painting depicting the Apotheosis of Saint Ann hung, wrinkled and cracked in its tarnished gilded frame. Gaspar jumped back as a large rat scurried out from behind one of the sarcophagi, ran through the open door, escaping into the garden.

Moving his light to the left of the open door, Gaspar froze as the beam landed on the distorted face of a very dead body sprawled on top of the seat built into the deep reveal. The shadowy alcove was partially hidden by the open door, and this new revelation startled Gaspar half to death.

With a blood-curdling scream, Gaspar jumped backwards, falling hard against Timmy Sullivan's sarcophagus behind him. Mouth agape, he stared from across the room for what seemed like an eternity at the still decomposing body which stared right back at him with empty eye sockets. The sight was horrific, as the corpse seemed to be screaming in terror from its own twisted, gaping mouth, a horrible tortured expression spread across what was left of the dead man's face.

This is a nightmare, Gaspar thought. *Who was this person, and what is he doing outside of a coffin?*

Gaspar slowly moved the narrow beam of light down the decaying carcass of the man. The cadaver still had wisps of hair on his head, and skin on his bones, but it also looked as if rats had been feasting on his flesh for a while too. Gaspar determined from the gruesome decay that that this person had obviously not died recently, but also evident that he hadn't been dead for years either.

Hot saliva filled his mouth and he knew he was going to puke, and hoped he wouldn't faint, but he was so light-headed from the stench. Swallowing hard, Gaspar got hold of himself, realizing that his entire world was about to turn upside down! Wanting to get outside before he passed out, he gathered all his strength and forced himself to move, stumbling back out into the sunlight.

Without waiting to catch his breath, he pressed 911 on his phone while simultaneously yelling at the top of his lungs for Jason.

Hearing the panic in his friends voice, Jason came running from where he'd been working in the carriage house. Arriving on the scene, the antiques dealer watched in wide-eyed disbelief, while his ashen-faced friend made his urgent call to the police.

"Hello, This is Gaspar Brown," he blurted out between short breaths, "Tell Captain Morgan That I've found A Dead Cadaver-Body at the old Sullivan mansion on Via San Marco." He took another short breath, looking Jason in the eyes as he spoke. "That's right, um-hmm … Yes, please ask him to send some officers, and the Coroner as quickly as possible." He swallowed hard. "I'm waiting here now." His voice cracked as he urged the operator to action before hanging up.

"Gaspar, what's going on?" Jason listened to Gaspar's emergency call with disbelief.

Gaspar just held out his hand like a traffic cop at an intersection, begging his friend to wait. His next urgent call was to his lawyer and future stepfather, Peter Cawthorne. Gaspar told him without any further explanation to, "Come to the Sullivan place … fast!" then hung up without even saying goodbye.

Jason proclaimed, "Another, *Dankish, Dread-Bolted, Death Token*," he could barely get the words out, "A *Dead Cadaver-Body*? WHERE?" The antique dealer was visibly shaken.

"Right here inside the mausoleum!" Gaspar blurted out, taking a deep breath while pointing to the open door of the tomb. It's the scariest thing I've ever seen, Jason." He shook off the memory. "My first Dead Cadaver-Body, TOO." He informed his pal, closing his eyes and shaking his head. "Bending over, Gaspar held his knees while sucking in great lungful's of air, like an Olympic athlete who'd just run the 1,500 meter.

"What should we do?" Jason had never had to deal with human remains before.

"Just wait," Gaspar caught his breath, "the cops are on their way." Gaspar assured him, taking another deep breath hoping to calm his nerves before the authorities arrived and All Hades broke loose.

It wasn't long before they heard approaching the house. Gaspar and Jason girded their loins and walked to the front of the house to let in the powers that be. First to arrive on the scene were Sergeant O'Malley, two officers, and a pair of paramedics with an ambulance. Peter Cawthorne arrived on their heels, wide-eyed at all the commotion.

"Peter, am I ever happy to see you." Gaspar said. "Thanks for coming Sergeant O'Malley. Follow me fellas." Gaspar told the assembled men who had come to take care of this gruesome business for him.

Gaspar, with Jason in tow, led them around the main house and through the guest house to the mausoleum. The police handled the nasty cadaver in an efficient, business-like way, but Gaspar wasn't going to wait around and watch. After showing the assembled officers, as well as Peter and Jason where it was, he got out of there in a hurry followed by the timid antiques dealer who tossed his cookies in the bushes the minute he hit fresh air.

"Let's just stay here, Gaspar insisted to Peter who left the mausoleum hot on Jason's heels. When Jason, still white and shaken, finally emerged from the rhododendron, Gaspar scooted over onto the garden bench he and Peter occupied and motioned for Jason to join them.

As the three friends waited solemnly out in the fresh air, the police and paramedics exited the building, carrying a stretcher with the dead body, fortunately covered by a long white sheet.

"What do you make of it, Sergeant O'Malley?" Peter stood up.

"Have you any idea how long the victim's been dead?" Gaspar asked his uniformed pal.

"Do you think he died of natural causes?" Jason could barely get the words out.

"The coroner will perform an autopsy. I'm sure Captain Morgan will fill you gents in with any details you need to know." For now I think this mausoleum is off limits to any further visits, until we complete our investigation." The sergeant insisted without disclosing any information.

"That won't be a problem, Sergeant." Gaspar promised. "It'll be a long time before I ever feel like going back in there, I can tell you that." He assured the officer.

"That goes double for me," Jason reiterated, "I hope I never have to see anything like that again, ever!" The antiques dealer was emphatic.

"I think I may have also discovered the death room." Gaspar told the sergeant, to Peter and Jason's looks of complete surprise.

"Where?" Sergeant O'Malley was skeptical.

"Upstairs, in the grooms' quarters, over the stables." Gaspar was matter-of-fact.

"Jason, send your guys through the tunnel to the upstairs of the carriage house and have them unseal the door leading to the upstairs from the motor court so that Sergeant O'Malley can get in from there. After that, I suggest you close up the house for the night." Gaspar said. "This has been quiet a day for all of us. You should probably send your crew home and also go home yourself."

"I'm with you, Gasp. I'm out of here." Jason agreed, "I'll lock up and see you tomorrow or whenever," he said. "I'll get that door open in the carriage house and then quit for the day." he told them, heading towards the house to give his men instructions, and to turn out the lights and lock up.

After Sergeant O'Malley and his men were done looking around the interior of the mausoleum, Gaspar closed the door and locked it, giving Sergeant O'Malley the key so that he could continue his investigation at will.

"Follow me Sergeant. This way to the Carriage house, men." Gaspar instructed, leading the way through the service yard to the door leading upstairs which Jason's men had just finished clearing.

Heading upstairs, the teenager led the authorities and Peter into the dorm room where the Sullivans' grooms or servants would have slept. "It's the last bed, Sergeant. The one under the window. I think it's d-d-d-ried blood." Gaspar stuttered.

O'Malley pulled back the covers and shook his head sadly. "This is definitely not good, Gaspar. There has been foul play here," he agreed. We'll need to secure this building and investigate further. I fear you're right, Gaspar. This is definitely a crime scene."

"I'm not sure if this is important or not, Sergeant, but if you look in that drawer by the bed, you'll find a loaded pistol inside." Gaspar informed them.

"Gaspar, how long have you known about that gun?" Peter asked.

"I discovered it about an hour ago, when I discovered the bloody bedclothes. I would have told you about it sooner or later … it's just that the dead cadaver-body made it sooner than later." Gaspar felt like a little kid explaining his actions to Big, Bad, Businesslike, Peter.

Sergeant O'Malley spoke up as they left the room. "I'll post men at the house all night to watch this building and the mausoleum to make sure nobody enters to tamper with evidence, if you don't mind, Gaspar and you too Mr. Cawthorne." He informed Gaspar and his attorney as they walked down the stairs to exit the building. "That's all we can do here tonight, boys. I suggest we close up and call it quits for today." He told his men and Gaspar when they were back outside again.

Just then, La Mar pulled up in the woody with the freshly groomed Mr. Peugeot looking out the window from the back seat.

"Goodnight Sergeant, goodnight Peter. I'll check in with you guys tomorrow," Gaspar promised, jumping into the back seat of the car.

"Goodnight, Gaspar. Don't let this worry you, everything's going to be alright." The kind Sergeant assured the still distraught teenager, closing the passenger door behind him while Peter waived through the car window.

"Where's Rajeev?" Gaspar asked the driver as he jumped in and hugged Peugeot.

"I'zz bin a-waitin on him fo ova an-owa, Suh." La Mar drawled. "I done lef him at de druk-sto an-owa ago. La Mar insisted. Ah coo-int wai no longa Suh, so azz come to git you now." La Mar explained, Rajeev's absence.

"I hope nothing's happened to him," Gaspar was concerned, while Peugeot kissed him effusively, washing Gaspar's face with his wet tongue.

"Wha be goin' on hea, Suh." La Mar asked as Gaspar got into the car. Wha-da poe-leez doin' hea?"

"I've just found a dead cadaver-body, in the mausoleum, La Mar. Gaspar whispered to the driver. There's also evidence that the victim was probably murdered upstairs over the carriage house." Gaspar told the driver, wiping his mouth after Peugeot put his tongue in it.

"A Det-Bowdi! Weez got-a git owta hea fast, boss." La Mar yelped, burning rubber in his panicked attempt to make a quick getaway.

Gaspar had to laugh seeing La Mar's expression in the rear view mirror. The drivers eyes were almost popping out of his head. As the car careened away from the death house, he told Peugeot, "I'm glad you weren't there boy, it was a *Guts-Griping, Hell-Hated, Reeling-Ripe, Rude Growing, Reeky-Rank, Puking, Maggot-Pie, Mess!*" Gaspar exclaimed, nearly retching at the thought of what he'd found.

Peugeot gave his master a knowing look before curling up and placing his newly coifed head in Gaspar's lap.

CHAPTER 14

RAJEEV

THE NEWS OF THE DISCOVERY OF A DECOMPOSING BODY ON PERDIDO ISLE SPREAD LIKE WILDFIRE. ALL KINDS of speculation circulated at Karen's Café, as well as across the island, with talk of a serial killer on the loose and other silly notions, scaring residents half out of their minds. The coroner performed an autopsy and what he discovered was startling to Gaspar. The victim was a man, most probably Indian. He had stood only five-feet, tall, and weighed 165 pounds. He was an old man, at least 75 years old. According to evidence, the victim had been tortured before being murdered. The Coroner determined that the victim had been murdered in the bed where Gaspar discovered the bloodstained sheets, and his body moved to the mausoleum shortly thereafter.

The victim had been dead for over six months, suffered horrific slashings to his body and finished off by a final gunshot to the head, dying, as the coroner noted: *at the hands of another. No motive could be discerned.*

In the meantime, Rajeev had disappeared into thin air. Gaspar had notified the police and the servant had been listed as a missing person, but he was nowhere to be found. The entire situation became more mysterious with each passing day.

Gaspar continued to piece the information together as best he could. When the police were done with them, Gaspar had all the papers in the victim's trunk, and bedside table as well as all the papers and the book he'd found in the sitting room, brought to his office at La Rinconada. He wanted these documents close at hand, not only for safe keeping, but so that he could study the materials carefully at his leisure. To assist his quest, Gaspar, had Margaret Stewart hire an expert in middle eastern languages to translate what he'd found.

The next day, Professor Youssef, the Middle Eastern and Asian scholar from Coral County Community College whom Margaret Stewart had retained, arrived at La Rinconada. It didn't take long for the professor to translate the papers into English and lay the translations down in front of his young employer.

Gaspar and Peugeot couldn't wait to hear the Professor's report. Bounding into the room together hoping for insight, Gaspar hollered, "What can you tell us, Professor? We're crazy to know what those documents say and what language they're written in." Gaspar asked with expectation sitting down across from the desk, with Peugeot jumping into the chair right next to him, sitting at attention.

"As you can see Mr. Brown," Professor Youssef explained pointing at the translations laid out on the desk, "I've divided the papers into two separate stacks. The ones on the left are written in Hindustani. The ones on the right in Arabic. "These in the middle are their English translations."

"That's very interesting, who would have thought that Rajeev was bi-lingual." Gaspar mused, scratching Peugeots ears.

"These papers" Professor Youssef motioned to the stack on the left side of the desk, are the property of a very devout Hindu. There is nothing of special interest here. Just general information, housekeeping notes, nothing out of the ordinary." The Professor discounted the documents as worthless. "They are written in the Devanagari script. Hindustani, standard Hindi and Urdu are usually written in this script, sometimes the Brahmi script is used, but not often. Hindustani orthography is derived from the script of Ancient India."

Gaspar looked at Margaret Stewart who was standing near the professor and nodded with understanding.

"Most Urdu texts are written in the Urdu alpha-bet, which comes from the Persian alphabet which is probably why you couldn't tell the difference between the two scripts used on these two very different stacks of documents."

Peugeot let out a loud yawn and licked his lips while Gaspar shook his head in the affirmative.

"The Devanagari script is an *abugida*, as written consonants have an inherent vowel, which in Standard Hindi is a *schwa*. In certain contexts, such as at the end of words, there is no vowel, a phenomenon called the schwa syncope. Other vowels are written with a diacritic on the consonant letter. Devanagari is written from left to right, with a top-bar connecting the letters together." The Professor pointed out, showing Gaspar and Margaret some of the Urdu script written on one of the documents that looked like so much chicken scratchings

अ आ ई उ ऊ ए ऐ ओ औ.

"That's too bad," Gaspar sighed, "I'd hoped there was something here that would be more revealing." He said sadly, petting Peugeot's back.

"On the other hand, young sir, these," the scholar said, pointing to the stack on the right and picking up the religious tome, "are the property of a very devout Muslim." Professor Youssef told Gaspar matter-of-factly. You have here a very well-read copy of the *Quran*." He said holding up the religious book that Gaspar had found in the sitting room.

"The *Core-Ann?*" Gaspar blurted out in plain English. "I thought Rajeev was a Hindu?."

"Rajeev is a very popular Hindu name, in India." The Professor told him. "But this book is the *Holy Quran*, the Islamic sacred book. This Holy Book contains the word of God as dictated by the Angel Gabriel, and written down in Arabic by Muhammed," the professor explained. "This book touches on all aspects of human existence, including matters of doctrine, social organization, and legislation."

"How do you spell that?" Gaspar asked grabbing a pad and a pen from the desk.

"Quran, Q-U-R-A-N," the professor told him. "It's also spelled K-O-R-A-N in the west and by the way, it's pronounced kor-AHN. It is also referred to in Arabic as al-Qurān and it's written in Arabic like this." He said grabbing the pen out of Gaspar's hand and drawing the following characters, القرآن, on the pad. Quran literally means, 'the recitation' and it's believed by Muslims to be a revelation from Allah, you know, God." He explained to Margaret Stewart, Gaspar, and Mr. Peugeot, who listened intently to Professor Youssef's every word.

"I get the picture, Professor," Gaspar assured the scholar, looking Peugeot in the eyes while nodding his approval.

"All of these other papers are also written in Arabic." Professor Youssef continued. "For the most part they discuss the invasion of the Indus Valley in India by the

Muslim Moghuls way back in the 14th century … around 1526 to be exact. This is a list of the spoils of war, taken from the Hindu's at that time," the Professor explained, holding up one of the documents, handwritten in Arabic.

"That's very interesting!" Gaspar exclaimed sitting bolt upright. "Was there any particular 'spoil of war' highlighted or mentioned more than once?" *Now we're getting somewhere*, he thought suddenly riveted.

"Something called the *'The Prism of the Sun,'* but there's nothing written here that says what *The Prism of the Sun* actually is." The Professor shook his head negatively.

"Oh, I see." Gaspar sat back in his chair, disappointed. "That's too bad," he mumbled under his breath right into Peugeot's left ear.

"Of course you know that the Indus Valley was previously conquered by the Achaemenid empire, under Darius of Persia in 516BC when they annexed parts of the Punjab west of the Indus River and Sindh." the Professor said presumptuiously, indicating he assumed neither Gaspar or Margaret could not possibly know what he was talking about.

Of course," Gaspar said calmly, "King Darius of Persia? It's the Naqshe-e-Rostam inscriptions, if I'm not mistaken, which heralds Darius as Aryan. "Let's see," he squinted his eyes deep in thought trying to remember exactly what Madame Martinez de Gozz had told him in Buenos Aires over Christmas vacation. Remembering his Argentinian friends exact words he began to chant as if in a trance:

"I am Darius, the great king, the king of kings the king of many countries and many people the king of this expansive land, the son of Wishtaspa of Achaemenid, persian, the son of a Persian, 'Aryan', from the Aryan race."

Gaspar was amused to see the looks of astonishment and disbelief on the faces of not only Margaret Stewart and Professor Youssef, but Mr. Peugeot, too.

Regaining his composure, The Professor swallowed hard, and piped up. "I'm afraid that's all I have to report, Mr. Brown." He confessed as he nervously packed up his briefcase.

"Thank you very much, Professor. Your input has been invaluable." Gaspar shook the old man's hand. "Mrs. Stewart will take care of your fee, and see you out. I have to go now myself, so please excuse me." Gaspar said while grabbing the stack of papers written in English off the desk as he headed out the door, Peugeot prancing along behind him.

It wasn't until the following Saturday that Gaspar and Peugeot returned to the scene of the crime. He had already formulated his plan of action before letting himself into the house. He wanted to look in the library. There were some albums there that he needed to study. With assurance he strode into the wood-paneled room and walked directly to the bookshelf that held the Sullivan Twin's, personal photograph albums. He had only glanced at these cursorily, but now he needed to really give them the once over. Choosing the album dated 1955, he perused the many photographs that the twins had glued into the album. There were pictures of them in safari clothes, taken in a desert setting. Several photo's showed the twins with a native guide. *Could that be Rajeev?* Gaspar wondered even though the young man in the photo had no resemblance to the old Indian servant, still missing. Looking through albums for the succeeding years up until 1960, he discovered more pictures of the twins taken with a servant in Indian garb and some of just the servant. Finally one of these was identified as Rajeev. Lining up all the photographic evidence chronologically, across the desktop, Gaspar grabbed an ivory handled magnifying glass and really studied the face and features of Rajeev. Although over fifty years had passed since the photographs had been taken, he could clearly tell that the Rajeev in the photographs, and the Rajeev he knew and who was now missing (somewhere in Florida or God knows where,) were not one and the same person. Rajeev's eyes were much further apart than those of the man in the photograph, and the shape of the missing Rajeev's face was more oval, where the man in the pictures had a round face. Compared to the Sullivan Twins, the man in the photographs was not at all tall ... but the Rajeev that he knew was at least five-foot-eight-inches tall. It didn't take a genius to realize that the man in the photos and the man who called himself Rajeev and who talked in Spoonerisms, were two completely different people. Gaspar knew what he wanted to do next. It was already part of his plan for today.

Having thoroughly searched the basement and the tunnels, and the first and second floors of the house, and of course the carriage house last week, his goal today was to search the servants' quarters on the third floor, under the eaves, way up in the attic. To this end he and Peugeot climbed the back servants' staircase of the mansion to the top floor of the house. Slowly he checked each room, hoping to find a trapdoor or secret panel that would open and reveal the Sullivan Twins' secret hiding place … but try as he might, he didn't find any. The layout of the rooms looked normal, but Gaspar began to get the feeling that he'd missed something.

Retracing his steps, he came back into what would have been the major domo's office. When Peugeot began to bark madly at the back wall of the closet, Gaspar took a closer look. That's when he found it. Searching one more time inside the closet, he found a secret panel that opened reluctantly after Gaspar finally determined where the mechanism was that triggered the release of the locks. "Good work, Peugeot," he complimented his pup as they watched in awe when the entire back of the closet swung free revealing a large square room, completely papered in a fussy wallpaper entirely covered in pink cherry blossoms. "This wallpaper wouldn't have been my first choice, not in a million years," he told Peugeot who ran into the room, barking furiously.

Gaspar was shocked to see that the room was empty—completely empty—swept clean. Considering that the rest of the house had taken Jason four weeks to clear of trash, it was surprising to Gaspar that the twins hadn't also trashed this large square room. He was baffled by their lack of interest in this secret room as he followed Peugeot into it for a closer look around. *Maybe they didn't even know it existed?* He considered the possibility, but without conviction.

It was a large, square, low ceilinged room. That's when the light bulb turned on in Gaspar's brain. Having already scoured all the other servants rooms on this floor, he wondered, *Why does this one have a lower ceiling than all the others?* He also asked himself, *Why is it square?* "This room should be rectangular," he told Peugeot, basing his assumption on the placement and size of the other attic rooms surrounding it.

Peugeot was circled the room, sniffing up a storm until finally he stopped in the middle of the left hand wall. Jumping up on his hind legs the clever dog, started barking again, turning his head, calling his master. That's when Gaspar also saw what the French poodle had discovered. "Good boy, Peugeot!" he complimented the pooch while getting down to business.

A hairline crack along one of the seams in the wall-paper revealed what could only be a secret door, but try as he might, he couldn't find the lever that promised to unlock it. Getting up on his tip-toes he ran his hands over the wallpaper. Finally he felt the slightest of tiny imperceptible bumps … a perfectly round little bump, high up off the ground. He could see now that it was a little pink-painted bump, placed right in the middle of one of the pale pink cherry blossoms of the busy wallpaper. This is it, he told himself as he gave the little bump a big push with the tip of his index finger.

WHOOSH!!!

The door swung backward into the room with the force of spring loaded hinges, knocking Gaspar down, pushing him over backwards, as a mountain of heavy jagged rocks EXPLODED downwards, threatening to bury him.

Peugeot, sprang aside, barking loudly as Gaspar instinctively rolled to his right while simultaneously pushing himself away from the booby-trap, wriggling away with determination from the avalanche on his butt!

Close one, he thought to himself, shaking off his surprise at having triggered yet another of the twins' murderous obstacles. "That was a close one, Peugeot. Are you alright?" he asked the pup who dashed over to his prone body and licked his face in reassurance. Gaspar put his arm around Peugeot's neck, pulling him in close. After they'd both calmed down, Gaspar let out a string of expletives, letting Peugeot know exactly how he felt.

"Of all the *Blue-Blistering, Blundering, Bird-Brained, Balderdash*!" He Captain Haddocked at the top of his lungs. "Those *Blithering, Bell-Bottomed, Black-Hearted, Bombardier's*!" He cursed the Sullivan Twins yet again. "You guys have tried to kill me and my puppy for the last time!" He told them off in no uncertain terms as loudly as his shaking voice could emote. "You *Double-Dealing, Tin-Hatted-Tyrants*," Gaspar yelped yet again. "You *Two-Timing, Toffee-Nosed, Traitorous-Twins*," he pounded the palm of his hand on the floor still not having satisfied his anger. "You haven't got me and Peugeot down yet." He yelled, shaking his fist heavenward. "You haven't licked us yet, and you haven't seen the last of us either, you *Two-Timing, Troglodyte, Tramps, Turncoats, TWINS!*" Gaspar was insistent on having the last word, and Peugeot wagged his tail in approval. He continued mumbling even more colorful curses under his breath as he got up and brushed dust off himself and Mr. Peugeot. Stepping carefully over the rubble, he cautiously walked through the open doorway, found and flipped on a light switch. What was illuminated was a staircase, leading upwards.

Gingerly, Gaspar and Peugeot climbed slowly upwards, step by step, half-expecting another dirty trick from the twins. As they reached the landing, Gaspar couldn't believe his eyes. Spread out before him was a large high ceilinged room, much larger than the room he'd just left below. The dramatic, pyramid shaped ceiling was built into the rafters of the house's high mansard roof. The entire room, walls, ceiling, and floor had been gold-leafed and lacquered. Hanging from the high ceiling were no less than five extraordinary crystal chandeliers, the kind he'd seen in photographs of Maharaja's palaces in India. Placed ceremoniously around the room were statues of Hindu gods and goddesses, as well as gilded carvings, and priceless objects studded with jewels and displayed under glass. Another glass case, stood in the center of the room. Under the glass box, on a plinth covered in golden velvet, stood a small stand on top of which lay a fitted pillow on which nestled the largest faceted red gemstone, Gaspar had ever seen.

"A pigeon blood Burmese Ruby of the first order," Gaspar whispered to Peugeot who stood up on his hind legs to see what his master was drooling over. He said this to the pup romantically, since he had no idea if it were a ruby, a rubellite, a carbuncle, a specitite garnet or a spinel. He just hoped it wasn't glass. He wanted to remove the case and touch the stone but stopped short, remembering what had happened to Indiana Jones when he picked up the golden idol in *The Temple of Doom*.

Peugeot began a low, rumbling, angry growl which turned into a fit of ferocious barking, causing Gaspar to shift his attention away from the mesmerizing gem.

"So fou've yound... I mean, you've found," he corrected himself, "IT," Rajeev's distinctive sing song voice startled Gaspar as it emanated from the direction of the staircase.

Gaspar whirled around, and saw Rajeev, looking at him with wild flashing eyes. The madman was wielding a knife. "Rajeev! Where have you been, what are you doing with that knife? We've been looking all over for you! Point that blade in another direction please. Why are you wearing that crazy skull-cap instead of your turban, and why are you growing a beard all of a sudden?" Gaspar was confused by the change in the servant's look and demeaner.

"AAHMAD. My name is Aahmad. It seems you've already found Rajeev," he snarled, "and I see that you've found *The Prism of the Sun*, too. Thank you very much." The servant smiled grotesquely.

"Aahmad?" Gaspar wasn't thinking clearly, until the truth of the situation suddenly dawned on him. "You *Murderous Muslim*, You Killed Rajeev!" He shouted lunging at the culprit but Gaspar's four-foot, eleven-inch, ninety-pound frame was no threat to the larger, stronger man who brushed the teenager aside as if swatting at an insect. When Peugeot bravely took up the attack, the Muhammedan kicked him and sent the stalwart canine skidding toward Gaspar lying on the floor. Grabbing his whimpering pet, Gaspar held him close, looking up at the knife wielding fiend. Now it was Gaspar and Peugeot's turn to listen.

"I've searched for this stolen stone for *yany mears* … many years," he frustratedly corrected himself. My *bearch srought* me to Perdido Isle many months ago." In his excitement he couldn't help but garble his words. I befriended Rajeev, the *souse hervant*, but he wouldn't tell me where the *hewel was jidden*." He rolled his eyes in frustration with his speech impediment and stamped his foot on the floor. "I *hortured tim*, and he still wouldn't tell. One day, I'm afraid I tortured him a little too much." The killer confessed sheepishly having finally gotten control of his Spoonerisms. "I humanely shot him in the head to put him out of his misery."

Gaspar couldn't believe that the madman actually prided himself on his charitable act towards an old man who he'd relentlessly tortured then butchered. "You'll have to pay for that Rajeev or Aahmad or whatever your name is." Gaspar informed him. "I'll have to turn you in." Gaspar threatened the murderer, still holding Peugeot who'd stopped whimpering and started growling again.

"No, you won't. I don't enjoy killing little boys, but if I have to, I will, and your satanic little dog too. I searched everywhere in this cursed house, but couldn't find it. I thanked Allah when you came along and so conveniently cleared out all the trash for me. I was certain I would find what I was looking for then, but try as I may, I could never find this cursed room. I have you and your devil dog to thank for leading me to this secret chamber. As of this moment, you may consider this gilded room, YOUR TOMB." He threatened Gaspar coldly.

"The jewel is yours, Aahmad. May you never have a day's luck with it." Gaspar cursed the stone and its would be robber.

"I suggest you just sit there quietly while I retrieve the jewel. If you do as I say, you nill wot be harmed, although it is my plan to lock you in this secret room for eternity. Now do as you're told boy ... scoot back, over there, by the statue of Kali, and control that mutt of yours, because if he *lets goose* ... I'll kill him." The madman didn't even attempt to correct his garbled threat.

Gaspar reluctantly did as he was told, holding Peugeot close. Scooting backwards from where he'd fallen on the floor, he retreated to the corner of the room, where he and Peugeot sat huddled together under the looming statue of Kali, Goddess of the Underworld.

"Before you disappear forever, Aahmad, tell me how you learned about the The Prism of the Sun. Tell me the history of this mysterious jewel, please," Gaspar begged. "After all, if I'm going to die here because of that cursed stone, I'd like to die with the knowledge of what this is all about." Gaspar insisted hoping to buy a little more time before being entombed for eternity.

"I am from the Indus Valley." Aahmad started, "My people conquered the city of Rappa several times, throughout history and this jewel, *The Prism of the Sun*, was part of our bounty. Rajeev's people, the dirty Hindu's, reconquered Rappa and took back the stone on more than one occasion before the city was lost forever. These

Sullivan Twins discovered the lost city and the Hindu temple in the 1950s. They stole what was rightfully ours as a spoil of war, *The Prism of the Sun*, and in doing so, they killed my father who had claimed the temple and protected it for our people. The Sullivans' Hindu servant, Rajeev was complicit in their crime and took their secret with him in death. I vowed to recover the stone and return it to my people. I intend to donate this valuable artifact to the Great Mosque of Mecca, the Sacred Mosque of Masjid al-āarām from where it can never be pillaged again! It is the largest Mosque in the world and it surrounds Islam's holiest place, the Kaaba in the city of Mecca, Saudi Arabia." Aahmad bragged. "Does that satisfy your curiosity, you insignificant infidel?" Aahmad finished with an evil smirk.

"It will do." Gaspar told him, "Carry on then, Aahmad. Do your worst." He gave the thief permission to steal the jewel from him and watched as Aahmad approached the plinth holding the apocalyptic stone. "By the way, is it Ratnaraj, the king of stones, or is it an apocalyptic stone? Gaspar asked.

"What are you talking about? *The Prism of the Sun* isn't a biblical stone if that's what you mean." Aahmad was getting testy.

"I'm only asking, if it is a Burmese Ruby?" Gaspar asked again.

"Oh, I understand. Ratnaraj? Not at all, and it's not one of those silly apocalyptic stones they talk about so much in the bible either." Aahmad told him dismissively. "It's THE LARGEST RED DIAMOND IN THE WORLD, priceless beyond all value, KING AMONGST THE KINGS OF GEM STONES." Aahmad informed his next victim condescendingly in a derisive, mocking tone. "If you had looked at it closely you would have seen The Holy Words of Allah, which HE HIMSELF carved into the stone, FROM THE INSIDE OUT!" Aahmad, revealed the presence of the stone's mysterious inscription with great pride and self-satisfaction, before turning away, removing the glass box and plucking the extraordinary red diamond, *The Prism of the Sun*, from its velvet pillow.

A split-second before Aahmad reverently plucked the stone from its velvet perch, Gaspar instinctively fell back against the statue of Kali assuming a fetal position while shielding his face with one arm and covering Peugeot with the other turning his body to protect the dog as much as possible as the enormous crystal chandelier hanging from the center of the room crashed to the floor, flattening the misguided criminal and scattering shattered crystal shards through the air and across the room.

When the explosion of crystal subsided, Gaspar jumped up along with Peugeot and ran over to where Aahmad was sprawled on the floor under the massive bronze frame of the elaborate light fixture. Gaspar first ascertained that the unlucky thief was still breathing before removing the diamond from the man's bloodied, but still clenched, fist. Peugeot stood guard, growling over Aahmad's prone body, while Gaspar took out his phone and called 911, followed by a call to Peter Cawthorne, and another to Jason Steinmeyer. For good measure, he sent a text to Alex, Kevin, and June, telling them to come over for the big finale to *The House of Mystery's, Mystery.*

• • •

Once again, the old Sullivan House was swarming with Perdido's finest, police, firemen, and paramedics. Gaspar met the first responders on the front porch and told them what they were going to find upstairs. "Follow me," he instructed the stretcher bearers as he lead the assembled authorities as well as his friends through the house. He took them through the closet, into the cherry blossom room, over the mountain of fallen jagged rocks, and through the secret door. "This way," he assured them as he charged up the stairs into the brilliantly gold-leafed attic space now strewn with shattered crystals. "There's your murderer, your thief, and your patient." Gaspar told the assembled officers, pointing to the prone body of Aahmad, smashed under the fin de siècle bronze Dore and crystal chandelier, still being guarded by the looming, growling, Mr. Peugeot.

It took four strong firemen and two big policemen to lift the bronze chandelier frame off of the moaning Muslim.

"Meet Aahmad, the murderer of Rajeev, the Sullivan Twins' innocent, loyal Indian retainer." Gaspar informed Sergeant O'Malley, Peter, Alex, Kevin, June, Brewster and Jason and the rest of the assembly.

"I thought his name was *Rajeev*?" O'Malley asked quizzically.

"No, Sergeant. The dead body-cadaver I found in the mausoleum the other day was Rajeev. This fiend tortured Rajeev before shooting him in the head so that he could assume Rajeev's identity. He confessed as much to me before triggering that booby-trapped chandelier. This crook's name is Aahmad. He's a Muslim. Rajeev was a Hindu. Rajeev was protecting a priceless jewel on behalf of the Sullivans. The jewel was a much-venerated religious artifact of the Hindus in India and apparently of Muslims around the world as well. That's why Rajeev was killed, and this ..." Gaspar explained opening his clenched fist, revealing the huge, sparkling red diamond lying in the palm of his hand, "was the object of Aahmad's desire."

Jason Steinmeyer stepped forward, eyes almost popping out of his head. "May I?" he asked politely, outstretching both hands, cupping them together to receive the flashing treasure.

"Be my guest, Jason." Gaspar humored the antiquarian, tossing the precious stone into his outstretched palms. "It's called The Prism of the Sun, Gaspar informed the connoisseur. "Check out the Arabic inscription carved inside the stone. Notice I didn't say on top of the stone, Jason. It's the word of Allah, and it's carved from the inside out."

"Just like the *Philosopher's Stone* in the Vatican," Jason marveled turning the stone over in his fingers, "but the one in the Vatican is an emerald." The antiquarian informed those who had gathered round to ogle the jewel he held in his trembling hands.

"It's from the famous lost city of Rappa." Gaspar told his pals. "It's not a ruby either. It's the world largest and most magnificent red diamond." The awed group turned their attention back to Gaspar. "The Sullivan Twins found Rappa *and* the lost Temple of Agneya dedicated to Agneya, daughter of the fire God Agni, and that stone way back in the 1950s."

"Wasn't that in the news not so many months ago?" June piped up. "Didn't I read recently that archeologists recently uncovered a lost city in the Indus Valley? I remember reading that what they found there was a 20-foot-tall statue of a goddess carved in red sandstone with a gaping hole in her forehead big enough to pitch a baseball through." June looked at the huge stone sparkling in the palm of Jason's hand then at Gaspar. When their eyes met, and she saw the ear to ear grin on

Gaspar's face, she realized that this was exactly what the newspapers had been writing about.

"I read that same article June." Gaspar corroborated her account. "You could help me out a lot Jason," he continued, "by finding out who's in charge of that dig. I think we should return that baby to its rightful owner, which if I'm not mistaken, will be the statue of Agni in Rappa. Besides, I've always wanted to take a trip to India. This little trinket gives us the perfect excuse." Gaspar chuckled and his young friends joined in the laughter.

Peter Cawthorne and his law clerk Brewster Wharton on the other hand, just shook their heads in disbelief as Alex, Kevin and June, shouted, "Please take us with you, Gasp!"

CHAPTER 15

HOUSE FOR SALE

That night, with Mr. Peugeot by Gaspar's side, a gala group gathered at La Rinconada for dinner. Gaspar and Peugeot had invited the whole gang, Alex, Kevin, June, his mom, Elvira and her fiancé, Peter Cawthorne, Peter's law clerk, Brewster Wharton, Jason Steinmeyer, and of course Felix and Angela were included too. All in all, it was a merry group that assembled around La Rinconada's big dining room table. Gaspar placed his mother on his right, and Peugeot on his left, sitting up in his very own armchair. Angela and Angelito had prepared the feast and two waiters from the Grand Hotel Floride were sent over to serve and clean up under Angelito's expert direction. As a special treat, Gaspar had placed the astounding 160 carat *Prism of the Sun*, in the middle of the dining room table, up on its Lucite plinth, nestled in the same pillow that had cradled it these many years while in hiding at the Sullivan mansion.

"Well Gaspar, that was quite an experience you and Peugeot had today." Peter breathed a sigh of relief. "What made you even think that there was a treasure like a big red diamond hidden in the old Sullivan mansion?"

"The twins were obviously scared for their lives, Peter. All those booby-traps! They were definitely protecting something. I just made it my business to find out what could be so valuable that it would be worth all that trouble?" Gaspar chuckled, and then came clean. "Actually, after we opened the vault in the library, I discovered a journal written by Tommy Sullivan in 1950, all about an expedition he and his brother Timmy and their Indian servant undertook to find the lost city of Rappa … and find it they did. The journal hints at treasure but doesn't spell anything out. I did my research right here in Uncle Charlie's library and found out enough about the legendary lost city to realize that the possibility of the Sullivans finding treasure there was high … and as you can see …" Gaspar gestured towards the red diamond in the center of the table, "it was!"

"What made you suspect Rajeev, Gasp?" Brewster asked.

"All of a sudden I got to thinking, just because he says he's Rajeev, doesn't mean he is Rajeev. And if he really isn't Rajeev, then who's body-cadaver did I find in the mausoleum?, What caused those horrible blood stains in the bed? It just didn't add up, so I searched around the library and found some old photographs of Rajeev taken in the 1950s and 60s … and it didn't take me long to realize that the dude in the photograph and the Rajeev that I knew were not one in the same person. I must admit, I was surprised when the dirty Muhammedan showed up in the treasure room, wielding a knife at me and Peugeot." Gaspar shuddered. You should have seen Peugeot attack the monster." He put his arm around the puppy's neck. "Peugeot is the bravest dog in the world. Yes, you are, Peugeot," he insisted rubbing his nose against Peugeot's shiny, wet, black muzzle."

"Gasp, you're too goofy about that hound," Alex told him jealously. "You'll spoil him if you keep treating him too much like a human."

"Al, the only kind of dog to have is a spoiled dog … and since I've never had a dog before, I think it's alright if I spoil Peugeot. After all, he's only one life away from becoming human, at least that's what I think. Peugeot … in your next life, you're gonna be a human … aren't you pal." Gaspar rubbed noses with his pup yet again.

"Wha da ya mean?" Alex was wide eyed.

"Well Al, us Hindu's, me and Peugeot that is … well you see … we believe in reincarnation, and so where I may come back as a Jellied Eel like you probably will too, Al … Peugeot here, will most likely come back as a spoiled French Prince … mark my words. Of course he'll have beautiful table manners too, just look at him, sitting up at table like I taught him. Have you ever seen anyone better behaved at table?" Gaspar laughed, kissing Peugeot on the mouth.

"Yuck, dog germs," Alex sputtered wiping his mouth reflexively.

"Did you really get the Mosquito to confess to the murder, Gasp?" Kevin took the spotlight off of Peugeot and Alex's feigned jealousy of him.

"Mosque-ito? His name was Aahmad, but that was a good one Kev." Gaspar complimented his friends wordsmithing. "Yes, the Mosque-ito confessed the whole business to me including his torture and murder of the real Rajeev."

"I'm surprised you didn't grab that diamond first! Alex chuckled.

"If I had, we'd be celebrating my funeral tonight instead of my triumph," Gaspar laughed, picking up the diamond and tossing it down the table to Alex who caught it midair with his right hand. "Thank God I like old movies. If you'd-a been paying attention when I showed you Indiana Jones and *The Temple of Doom*, Al, you'd have known like I did, that the diamond was probably more booby-trapped than the entire house. I guess Aahmad, like you … you *Beslubbering, Beef Witted, Mumblenews* … didn't pay attention to the movie either." Gaspar laughed.

"Well dear, what's your plan for the old house?" Elvira asked her son.

"I'm going to sell it … if anyone wants to buy it, and I think I'll subdivide the lot too. You know Al, there's enough land there to build another big house at each end of the property. You can help with the plans, since you're planning to be an architect when you grow up." Gaspar threw his pal a bone.

"Cool, thanks Gasp…" Alex said with appreciation.

"And I could help with the interiors …" June suggested shyly.

"Good idea June," Gaspar agreed.

"What about all the stuff inside the house, Gasp? Are you planning to keep any of it? Jason wondered.

"I'll leave that up to you, Jason. You know I'll want any first editions, unless I already have them here in my own library. The painting by Sargent is kind of a nice souvenir of the crazy Sullivans. I'd like to keep that, for sure. I'm not so crazy about the rest of the furniture or any of the knick-knacks. All the stuff I would have liked was broken up by the booby traps.

"I know," Jason lamented, "all that Coleport china, and the pineapple patterned crystal." He bemoaned, looking at Alex accusingly.

"Don't look at me, Jason," Alex whined, "I was nearly killed by all that old used junk."

"If you think there's anything worth keeping, Jason, just let me know." Gaspar jumped back in. "As for the statues and jeweled treasures up in the attic … I want those. We just have to find a place to display them around here." He added, "There must be some empty corner at La Rinconada we can find to put some Asian antiques. Maybe in the haunted room?" Gaspar suddenly had an inspiration. "Hey guys, that would make a great Oriental opium den kinda hang-out." He enthused, to his friends' looks of confusion.

"So when can we put the place on the market?" Brewster wondered, changing the subject.

"In a couple of months. I want to clear it out, paint it all white, update the kitchens and bathrooms, re-do the floors, and make sure that the gardens are in tip top shape before calling in the realtors." Gaspar had obviously been thinking about this for a long time.

"Here we go again …" Peter moaned.

"Get out the checkbook, Peter." Brewster laughed.

"Yeah, prepare yourself to be amazed." Gaspar had the last word.

• • •

Little did Gaspar know that *The Mystery of the Yucatan Legacy* would soon consume all of his spare time and imagination, pushing any pending real estate transaction or house building plans to the back burner.

Made in the USA
Las Vegas, NV
15 May 2022